Total-E-Bound Publishing books by Shermaine Williams:

Hot and Humid
How Sweet It Is
Lady in Red
Remote Control
Lean and Mean
Faultless Facade
Twisted Angel
Art of the Written Word
Two with a View

ART OF THE WRITTEN WORD

SHERMAINE WILLIAMS

Art of the Written Word
ISBN # 978-0-85715-439-2
©Copyright Shermaine Williams 2011
Cover Art by Lyn Taylor ©Copyright 2011
Interior text design by Claire Siemaszkiewicz
Total-E-Bound Publishing

Published in 2011 by Total-E-Bound Publishing, Think Tank, Ruston Way, Lincoln, LN6 7FL, United Kingdom.

Total-E-Bound Publishing is an imprint of Total-E-Ntwined Limited.

Manufactured in the USA.

ART OF THE WRITTEN WORD

Dedication

For those who like to buck the trend.

Chapter One

His body glistened in the blazing sun, water dripping from his dark hair onto his muscular chest. She followed the route of the droplets as they rolled down his smooth brown skin, catching the light as they navigated his defined abs. Soon, she found her gaze directed at his crotch.

"You should go in, the water's lovely and warm."

Looking up at the fine specimen, she felt her face colour with embarrassment, offering a tight smile as he walked past where she sat on the warm sand. Turning to watch him walk up the beach, a shiver of excitement shot up her spine as she saw him turn back to look at her, holding her gaze for several long moments.

She knew it was definitely going to be the holiday of a lifetime.

Yvonne stood at the door of her small home office, considering the young man as he in turn considered the plain, white wall. Tensely awaiting his verdict, her nails skidding across the glossy paint on the doorjamb, she almost felt the need to hold her breath.

Since his arrival, the atmosphere in the house had been different, charged with an energy she wasn't used to.

He looked much younger than she would have imagined, and the stirring thoughts that flooded her mind left her faintly self-conscious. He couldn't be more than twenty-five years old.

He was her gift to herself — or rather his services were — after getting her first romance novel, Holiday Pursuits, published. She had sought to hire an artist who would paint the book's cover as a mural on the wall of her study and, after a little internet research, she'd found Garvey. A man who, as it turned out, was over six feet of wiry muscle with slim dreadlocks hanging uniformly to his shoulder blades, the black interwoven with strands of sun-bleached brown.

Though it was overcast, he had chosen to cover his fit physique with only a T-shirt and long shorts, his dark skin on display beyond the thick khaki cotton. Yet it seemed appropriate, like he had brought the sun with him.

"I could do much more," he confessed, looking at the cover of the book she had given him. "Don't mistake me — this a nice picture, still — but I can do better."

She was almost mesmerised by his deep voice, to the point where she only heard snippets of what he actually said as he spoke of colours, size and originality as an argument against someone else's work.

His blended accent didn't know what it wanted to be, seeming to have picked up qualities from a number of different lands. The underlying West Indian lilt was unmistakable, though, reminding her of a childhood of climbing mango trees, tending to chickens and running down the lane to get a pink snow ice from Miss Marcy when her mum gave her a few cents. Her own history was unrecognisable from her clipped English tones, the result of many years of teaching English literature.

Everything he uttered came with a cool confidence, easily convincing her to agree to give him free reign. Simply being held in his gaze made her very aware of her own body, every slight feeling magnified as if she was being studied. "What do you have in mind?" she asked, overcoming her sudden shyness enough to advance into the room, relinquishing the support offered by the doorjamb.

Her loose muslin trousers, designed for comfort, seemed to become tighter with every step she took, clinging to her body as if they were shrinking. Heading for her desk, aligned with the wall across from where Garvey stood, every step seemed like a loud thud when her bare feet were in reality silent against the wood.

Simply being close to the familiar spot gave her comfort, lessening the risk of her collapsing on legs that had turned to jelly, though her temperature remained high. Even at a distance from him, she still found that his height forced her to angle her face upwards to look him in the eyes.

"Something original, that won't age—this image gon' look old quick. Maybe something personal to you."

Yvonne's brow furrowed, the nape of her neck prickling as she predicted the direction the conversation would take.

Turning to face her fully, Garvey raised the copy of her book. "I can borrow dis?"

Yvonne nodded, hiding the nerves she felt at the prospect of him judging her words.

"If you have any memorable experiences, I can recreate them in picture form."

"Memorable experiences?"

"You know, any special occasions between you and your partner." He raised an eyebrow questioningly. "Don't worry, I will keep your business private."

The warmth of faint embarrassment quickly spread up her chest and neck to reach her face. *Does he actually expect me to regale him with tales from my sex life?* "No, nothing like that."

There was something knowing about his easy smile, his high cheeks lifting further and accentuating the flash in his dark eyes. "That's all right, I can still give you a nice result."

"I'm glad."

Yvonne felt her body relax, leaning against the rear of her swivel chair, filled with relief at his acceptance of the commission. Impressed with every one of the paintings displayed on his website, she had set her heart upon him because he stood out from the rest. She would have been disappointed if she had been forced to choose someone else because he didn't want to do it.

Relief turned into a faint empty sensation as a sense of finality marred the meeting.

"Garvey, can I offer you a drink?"

The suggestion hadn't even occurred to her when he'd first arrived. Her attention had been occupied by the striking sight of the handsome man she found at her door.

Like his body, his face was slender. Highlighted by a strong jaw, each change of expression shifted the sinews beneath his creamy coffee complexion.

After she'd let him in, there had been a number of other aspects to become mesmerised by—his voice, his smile, the fluid movement of his body. He exuded a calm confidence, easily taking charge of the exchange without being overbearing.

She still held the postcard-sized image that he had offered as a business card, his contact details on the rear of a simple line drawing of a woman's profile, displaying a long and graceful neck. Holding it by the edges to avoid spoiling it with fingerprints, she led the way back downstairs to safely prop it on the tiled mantelpiece.

"Would you like a tea or coffee?"

Accepting her offer of a seat on the cream sofa, Garvey settled and looked instantly relaxed. "A cold drink for me, please."

"I have orange juice?" she offered, her brow furrowing as she thought about what else her fridge contained.

The broadened smile he offered along with a nod made him look even more youthful, increasing Yvonne's embarrassment at her inability to take her eyes off him. Nerves lightly fluttered in her stomach as she turned away, a strange sensation that didn't go away with the act of getting her guest his drink.

Being in a separate room gave her some relief, allowing her to take the deep breath that she had needed since he arrived.

Reaching into the fridge, she found her gaze drawn to her bare hand, unadorned by a wedding ring for over a year and a half. Since then, she had only dated a few men who were too much like her ex-husband for it to go anywhere. Still, she knew she had to move on, but certainly not with a man so young.

Pouring two glasses of juice, she took another deep breath, briefly considering the bottle of wine that she had bypassed before returning to the living room.

Garvey's demeanour was unchanged by her entry, barely looking up from the sketch book in his hand.

"There you go." Yvonne set the glass down on the table in front of him before sitting in the armchair opposite him.

"Thank you," he smiled.

"I also have some wine, if you'd like."

"I nah drink alcohol," he said distractedly, briefly looking up at her before returning to his pad.

With his document case lying on the coffee table, he was occupied solely by a sketch pad and a pencil.

"Are you sketching me?" she asked, seeing him repeat his quick glance up at her.

"You mind?"

She felt naked under his gaze, his apparent skill for looking inside her making a shiver run up her back. "Er, no."

"Inspiration." The word hung in the air, his deep voice somehow adding gravity to it.

Her attempt to relax only increased the tension in her muscles, making her sit straighter and press her toes into the carpet. Hoping she was sufficiently still, she fought the desire to reach up to pat her short black hair, gleaming and neatly brushed back, just long enough to secure in a clip.

In the silence, Yvonne was sure she could hear her own heart beating, making her wonder whether he could also detect it. The serene stillness did nothing to lessen her anxiety, only making it gradually build with every passing moment.

"Now I t'ink of it again, I find the main reason you better not to put this picture 'pon the wall."

As he spoke, his hand continued to move, blindly stroking the pencil across the page as he held her gaze, not needing to look down, like a skilled typist only watching the screen.

"You gon' run out of space quick when you nex' books come out."

Blinking rapidly, she thought back over their conversation to recall whether she had mentioned any other books, quickly concluding that she hadn't. "What makes you think there are going to be any more books?"

Turning over the cover of the pad, he put down the tools of his trade and looked at her with a new intensity, enough to make her reach up to self-consciously stroke her hair.

"I just know."

Though fairly taken aback by the definite reply, Yvonne did nothing to show it and stopped short of asking him what he meant.

"Can I see the picture?" she asked, satisfying a desperate need to fill the silence.

Grinning broadly, the accompanying glint in his eye provided a reply before he said a word. He shook his head. "No, this is for me. I will show you the ideas I have for your wall."

It was immediately apparent that pushing him would be futile, though a hint of mischief shining through his look of resolve suggested that he wanted her to press the point. Filled with a feeling of lightness, she couldn't help but smile at his teasing.

Taking a sip of her drink, she watched him over the rim of her glass, her relaxed state allowing her to look at him more closely. A hint of duskiness scattered across his jaw was created by a touch of stubble. Though she normally thought it scruffy, Yvonne liked the way it looked on Garvey. "How long have you been an artist?"

Though she already knew the answer after having studied his website, it was still a question worth asking — a subtle way of getting to hear his voice.

The plan worked, making Garvey talk about when he had first begun painting and his favourite media.

Eager to show that she was listening, Yvonne specifically asked about images she had seen on his website and how he decided what to paint.

"I get inspiration from everywhere," he replied. "People, life, music, sex."

Though she was unaware of it, her lips twitched at the final word. It wasn't a sign of a forthcoming response, witty or otherwise. Entranced, she found herself unable to speak.

Ordinarily, she was ultra-organised and possessed a natural ability to multi-task, which failed her completely when the topic of sex arose. The fact that she had penned a romantic tale about love and sex in a foreign country offered no comfort, as she had written it whilst alone.

The single word he uttered left her curious about his body, thoughts of what he was capable of overtaking her mind until visceral images played in her head like a silent movie.

The lithe and taut appearance of his body fuelled her imagination, making her picture the pleasure he could deliver. Despite having at least fifteen years on him, Yvonne had no doubt he had enjoyed some impressive experiences that would make him a good teacher.

"You must get inspiration from everywhere too."

A distinct feeling of discomfort came with his pause, a deafening indication that he expected her to respond. His openness was in contrast to her natural reserve. She was too staid to discuss personal matters, and certainly not with someone so young.

The fact that his self-assurance never gave way to arrogance increased his draw, making her automatically compare him to other men.

He held her gaze as he described the way skin gleamed as a subject moved their body, the positions into which a figure could be manipulated.

At that moment, she would have loved nothing more than to be the focus of his art, imagining creating the perfect pose to satisfy his need.

Her gaze flicked between his eyes and his lips as she listened to his words, warm and sensual like a tight embrace from a naked form.

From the way he spoke, it was difficult to tell whether he was talking about a model or a lover. Either way, she was sure that he somehow knew her mind, reading her with the intense look in his dark eyes.

"The body is a perfect subject for art because you have so many options. I can paint the entire form or take photos of shapes made by small parts of the body."

She watched his hand gestures, the movement of his face as he described the countless contours, silhouettes and shapes he'd discovered in the female form.

Whether purposely or not, his words made her more aware of her own body. She began unconsciously running her hand up her thigh as he described one of his favourite photographs—a close up shot of the valley where the thigh meets the bottom, displaying only a small fraction of the curve of the rounded cheek.

Curling her legs beneath her, Yvonne leaned against the chair arm as liquid heat flooded her pubis. Pretending nothing had changed, only her slightly parted lips betrayed her thoughts by releasing quickening breaths.

The realisation that photography fell within his artistic skills made her picture herself as his model, letting him physically put her into the position he desired, the strength and heat of his hands against her skin.

Her temperature increased as if the warmth of his hands created an imprint everywhere he touched, radiating outwards until every inch of her prickled with gradually growing heat.

The solid feel of his muscles would be felt every time he brushed against her, the smooth motion causing a frisson of pleasure to run down her spine.

In her mind's eye, he went further without hesitation, seeming to know what she wanted before she did. Each action created a more intense sensation, until she could almost feel the pressure of his embrace. Despite him being seated opposite her, she felt his considerable frame enveloping her entire body as if he wanted her to feel each of his developed muscles.

She would part her thighs to accommodate him, fitting perfectly against her like it was exactly where he should be. Even in her head, she could feel his body was unlike that of any other man she had experienced before, his skin smooth and taut with muscle.

Feeling the heat radiating from his skin as she squeezed his biceps, she would let her hands drift up his shoulders. His dreadlocks would swing with each movement, softly brushing her face as he positioned himself between her splayed thighs. His solid body would weigh against her, creating a satisfying pressure that sank her deeper into the unresisting sofa.

The sensation of being spread by his girth seemed a very real one, making Yvonne shift in her seat as he plunged deeper. Nodding as his lips moved, she remained unaware of what he was saying or whether the gesture was relevant.

Her body would open up to accept him, her folds yielding and her moisture aiding the passage of a shaft that seemed too big. The mere thought of what his body was capable of was enough to make her breath catch.

"You don't use your own experiences for book ideas?"

"Um, yes." A vein in her neck began to throb uncontrollably, making her hand drift upwards as if to hide the sudden affliction. "Some experiences can inspire a good story."

She mentally began to create the story he would inspire, the opening of an erotic tale forming in her mind, with the hero closely resembling Garvey. She had no doubt the book would take a significant amount of time to write — even if it was a short story, each chapter would certainly leave her spent. Rather than it simply being a story from which she was somewhat removed, she would experience every word.

Just by looking at him, she could tell he possessed a level of energy that would leave her exhausted and satisfied. She was sure that he knew more than she did, a few tricks to show off his prowess in commanding a woman's climax.

"What are you thinking about?" he asked after a pause. "You look deep in thought."

Jolted from her daydream, the realisation that he might have been watching her for an extended period mortified Yvonne.

"Er, nothing." The ridiculousness of the reply made her shake her head. "I mean, I was considering the similarities in our jobs. Both very creative."

With a slight nod, Garvey briefly pursed his lips as his gaze flicked to his sketch pad. "True."

Running her tongue across her own lips, she could only imagine how good it would feel to kiss him. What is wrong with me? she thought, berating herself over uncontrollable emotions. Garvey, of all people, raised feelings in her that had been absent for too long. It should be impossible, something that would never happen. But her mind refused to let go of its imaginings. Even with the touch of anxiety that arose with the thought of exposing her naked body to the young artist.

"All sorts of experiences can inspire you."

Only vaguely recognising what he said, hearing his voice as if he was trapped behind glass, she still nodded in agreement.

"Does that mean I'll find out something interesting about you when I read your book?"

Smiling shyly, Yvonne averted her gaze and turned her head, sure that he could read something in her expression. She thought about all the lustful encounters she had created between the fictitious couple, eventually leading to the heroine staying with her new lover, abandoning the idea of returning home from the tropical island.

The tale had been formed purely from her imagination, as Yvonne would never consider such a scenario—it was out of the question. Not sure of what light this would put her in, she wasn't keen on revealing it.

"Do you use your own experiences for your pieces?"

A beat passed before he replied with a smile. "I think it's hard to avoid."

Though she attempted to follow as he continued to muse the process from idea to conclusion, it proved difficult as her mind wouldn't allow her to concentrate on his actual words. Letting her gaze drift over his frame, she knew it would be easier if she couldn't see him.

She couldn't help but think about him in terms of the clandestine trysts she reserved for her characters. The vague idea of him inspiring a good hero disappeared as quickly as it arrived, giving way to the more intense and gratifying thought of her being his heroine.

It was easy to picture the two of them on a beach, a beautiful stretch of coast that was inexplicably deserted. She watched him emerge from the sparkling translucent blue water like the hero in an action movie, the sun making the clinging droplets glint like jewels covering his skin.

She would lay, waiting, the water dripping from his locks onto her body offering relief to her burning skin.

"...some things just deserve to be immortalised."

Yvonne slipped in and out of the present, mostly in time to catch a comment that required a response, nodding intermittently the rest of the time. Holding up her end of the conversation didn't prevent her seeing her own reclining form, feeling his weight against her until she sank into the sand.

The sensation of his shaft pressing against her thigh made her flinch, shifting in her seat to hide it. She crossed her arms over her chest, feeling as though her nipples were on display, despite her bra and T-shirt. With her thighs pressed together, she curled them up into her body, attempting to cease the rapid beat that suddenly began drumming between her thighs.

"I might ask you to model for me one day."

The assertion brought Yvonne back from being lost in the depths of her daydream, an unintelligible sound leaving her lips with a deep exhale.

Garvey's easy smile gave the impression that he understood the response, even though she didn't.

Studying his face, she trailed her gaze down from his heavy-lidded eyes, skimming over his straight nose to his mouth—a tempting pair of lips that offered her a kind smile.

Dusk had descended while the couple had been sitting there, leaving them in a fading light that softened their surroundings. Yvonne was surprised so much time had passed since he had arrived in mid-afternoon.

Unsure of whether she was being teased, she smiled back, curving her lips a little as if she knew what he was talking about.

"Already I have a few ideas, but I wan' show you some sketches first. I can come back day after tomorrow?"

"Sure, of course."

The response prompted him to get to his feet, which caused a distinct feeling of disappointment in Yvonne. Heaviness weighed in her chest, gradually lowering until a large heavy stone lay in the pit of her stomach. However, she stood as if nothing at all was wrong, maintaining a slight smile as she held his gaze.

As she took his proffered hand, the warmth of his firm grip spread heat through her body, dissolving the heavy pressure. Garvey held her hand longer than was necessary for a handshake, maintaining a firm grasp of her fingers as he looked into her eyes.

"I look forward to seeing you again."

A sudden yearning made her heart race, leaving her at the point of making up some random reason for him to stay. However, the only words that she was able to utter were, "Yes, me too." Suddenly, she felt the roughness of his barely-there stubble as his face stroked hers, making her marvel at her own imagination.

Letting go of her hand, he gathered his things before leading the way to the front door, which gave her a last opportunity to study him. She swiftly trailed her gaze up and down his frame, keen to drink him in completely before the chance was gone.

Reluctantly she followed him, still determined to play the good host despite the desire that coursed through her body like a rush of adrenaline.

"Have a good evenin', Miss Yvonne."

Hearing her name upon his lips made her smile, unsure whether that was the first time. "Thank you, Garvey, and you."

He returned her smile before opening the door. "I'll see you in a couple days."

In her head, she replied with words that were subtle and seductive, I'm looking forward to it. However, no words came.

Exhaling deeply as she watched him leave her home, she was almost relieved at his departure. She didn't know what the result would have been if he stayed much longer. After passing through the gate, he turned around to offer a final smile and a nod, just visible through the shadowy atmosphere into which he then disappeared.

Suddenly, she had a very good idea of exactly what would have happened if he had stayed. She'd been close to losing control simply from looking at him.

Yvonne's methodical habits would normally have left her concerned that nothing had been set in stone—the image hadn't been decided, she didn't know the cost, she didn't know how long would it take. Usually, she would have considered the situation too disorganised, but not one of those points now entered her mind as a problem.

Upon returning to the living room, she detected the subtle scent of his body that hung in the air like an invisible mist, a clean crispness that reminded her of a walk through a lush wood on a spring day.

Despite his absence, the atmosphere remained charged, emphasised by the fragrance that tickled her nasal passages, awakening her body from the slumber she hadn't known it was in.

After pulling at her shirt, suddenly too tight and feeling restrictive, she returned to the living room to pick up their glasses — his empty, hers still half full.

Chapter Two

As he raised his paintbrush, she watched the muscles in his shoulders shift and swell as he reached across the canvas. Unable to keep her eyes from drifting downwards, her gaze alighted on the cheeks of his toned bottom. Initially sure that he didn't know she was there, she began to have doubts as he set down his brush to pull his paint-splattered vest over his head. She gazed at the muscles in his back as he continued to work as if mesmerised, imagining her fingernails scraping along his dark skin. Suddenly, he turned around and saw her standing there.

"I'm returning you book," he confirmed, his dreadlocks falling over his face as he put down a battered and bulging black satchel. "I'm grateful you lend it to me."

His long cargo shorts rode up as he crouched down, perfectly balanced on the balls of his feet, bulging calf muscles on display as he looked for her book.

"You finished it already?"

Smoothly straightening to his full height, he steadily looked her in the eye as he held out the book. "Yes."

Along with surprise, a frisson of excitement flowed through her body, not only from the return of the mysterious artist, but also at the sight of all his equipment. Despite him only having reached the hallway, he seemed to change the atmosphere of the entire house to make it appear brighter.

She considered the possibility that it had something to do with the dreams that had filled her head for the last two nights — an extension of the thoughts he had unwittingly prompted with the power of his words.

The vivid dreams had developed from one night to the next, becoming more explicit after a day spent thinking about him through an exaggerated recollection. She imagined that they had been more familiar from the first moment they met, greeting each other with warm hugs and tender kisses.

She liked to think that, in her younger days, she could have been with a man like Garvey. He would have been her type at one point, which fuelled the pictures in her mind and the yearning of her body.

The night wasn't long enough for all the imaginings her unconscious mind wanted to create, the resultant intense sensations leaving her reeling when she awoke.

After exploring her body with his artistic eye, she pictured him taking advantage of it. Laying her down on the sofa, he would cast his admiring gaze over her one last time before covering her eager body with his.

"You ready?"

Her heart gave a single heavy thump before it seemed to stop, as she wondered what he was referring to.

"All right if I go upstairs?"

"Oh, yes, of course." Her fingertips tingled as though her blood had begun to flow again.

The smile on her face as she watched him ascend the stairs was one of slight awkwardness, as opposed to happiness. She knew, though he didn't, she had spent longer than usual preparing for his arrival, preening and carefully choosing a twin-set and skirt like it was a special occasion. It left her feeling foolish, shaking her head as she followed him up the stairs.

His failure to offer an opinion about her book hadn't escaped her notice, which made her wary of asking for one. Studying his face, Yvonne attempted to gauge his view purely by his expression. The pounding of her heart was for nothing as he looked completely at ease, as he had the day before.

Her book had been released two months previously, more than enough time for reviews to have been written, but it had been relatively easy to avoid them. She'd made a conscious decision that had been easy to stick to, until it came to Garvey.

It was suddenly essential that she know what he thought, adrenaline surging through her body and rolling down her back in a wave of heat. He withdrew a sketch pad larger than the one he had brought before. The action threatened to change the subject to the point of no return.

Quickly becoming convinced he had a criticism to make, the question burst from her mouth in a demanding manner. "What did you think?"

Garvey appeared unfazed by the query, despite his expression revealing he was aware of what she was talking about.

"Of my book, of *Holiday Pursuits*."

With a short, low hum and a smile, he proceeded to open his pad as he sat on the battered, brown leather sofa that occupied the entire wall of the study.

"It was very nice, well written."

She bristled, taking his words as code for boring.

Patting the seat next to him, he successfully beckoned her to his side, the innocuous gesture sufficient to automatically draw her to him.

"I thought you'd be more adventurous," he confessed, turning to look her in the eye. "Is jus' a bit tame."

"Tame?"

From anyone else she would have taken offence, but that proved impossible with Garvey. The smile that lit up his face held no malice, only a hint of mischief alongside his mild delight.

"The gentle way they met, all the timid glances," he explained. "I thought instant burning passion would have been more appropriate."

Though not keen on hearing more, Yvonne could only look at him expectantly.

"I was jus' expecting more after meeting you."

Watching his lips form the surprising words before looking back into his eyes, she searched their dark depths as if trying to read his mind. *What is he trying to say? Is that a compliment or an insult?* she mused. While she saw a sparkle in his eyes, it revealed nothing of what he really thought.

The need to prove him wrong rose in her throat, lodging there like a cork in the neck of a bottle and hindering her voice. Pressure built from the continuing desire to say something, making her body quiver as it sought a release.

Though it was unclear exactly what he'd been expecting, she was sure he thought her boring. No doubt he couldn't imagine that anybody her age could possibly be shy and retiring. She desperately wanted him to explain further but the words refused to come, leaving her only able to fix her gaze on his face, studying every minor movement.

Nothing about his demeanour suggested he recognised the fervent reaction he had caused.

Rather than elaborate, he turned some pages to show her the sketches, revealing the ideas that he had put down on paper. The casual manner in which he moved on from the comment caused resentment, felt as a gentle simmer in the pit of Yvonne's stomach.

He looked up at the canvas he would be decorating as he began to describe an image of two entwined figures. The richness of his voice made the smouldering bitterness subside, leaving only a warm contentment circulating through her body as she followed the picture he created with words.

His eyes danced about, as if he was already applying paint and following the flow of the lines across the wall. Briefly looking up to consider his view, Yvonne wasn't surprised that she was only able to see a blank wall, and transferred her gaze back to his face.

Sliding the sketch pad across to her lap, he let her see what was in his mind's eye as he continued to voice his ideas.

She pretended to have more interest in the image than she actually did, quickly taking in the rough drawing of two faceless forms in an embrace, preferring to watch the movement of his lips and eyes.

For a moment, she was lost in a fantasy that stemmed from his words despite barely being able to follow them. The picture that he verbally painted blended into her thoughts, becoming part of her imagination and drawing her more deeply into the idea of the couple being the real-life version of the sketch. The inspiration for his vision.

She had no qualms about letting him do precisely what he wanted to do—she'd known that from the first moment she met him. She would raise no objections to anything he wanted to create on the wall.

As he spoke of the flowing lines that would create the illustration of the figures twisted together, she imagined his hands trailing along the curves of her own figure. She saw herself lying on her side, feeling the heat from his hand as it stroked the valley of her waist and over her hip. Tracing the tips of his fingers up from the crease beneath her bottom, he gradually moved higher until his feather-light touch tripped across the small of her back.

The imagined sensation felt real enough to make her flinch as a shiver ran up her spine.

"You okay?" He interrupted his oration to turn to her, displaying a slight look of concern in his eyes.

"Yes," she instantly replied, nodding enthusiastically. "I'm fine."

Apparently satisfied, Garvey switched to more practical matters and explained what materials he would use and how long it would take, before asking if she was happy. It served to break the spell that held Yvonne, making her automatically respond with what he wanted to hear. "Sure, it all sounds great."

As he took the pad from her lap, his fingers stroked her thigh, making her body tremble as she wondered whether it was a deliberate act. Her gaze followed him as he got to his feet, her heart becoming heavy as she watched him empty equipment from his bag.

For a moment, she couldn't take her eyes off him, intently watching every action as if they were something new and wondrous, rather than simply unpacking. Surprised by the wide range of professional-looking equipment he produced, she realised she had expected his manner of working to be somewhat more casual. The paintbrushes, pencils, small pots of paints and other implements that she didn't recognise made the bag seem bottomless, able to make a never-ending supply of tools materialise.

"You sure you like the idea?"

Yvonne, mesmerised by a colour palette he had withdrawn, dragged her gaze from the sheet of card that displayed a spectrum of hues. Looking up, she found him considering her closely as if able to detect signs of a lie.

Suddenly, her throat became dry enough to make her swallow hard before replying. "Absolutely."

His knowing smile arose faster than her reply had been uttered, lighting his face as the paint-splattered drop cloth in his hand partly unfurled. "What about it you like most?"

The unexpected question left her speechless as she tried to recall his words rather than her fantasy. It came back to her hazily, only a few minor details that were insufficient to allow her to respond in a knowledgeable way.

His deep rolling chuckle flowed from his lips to fill the room, surrounding Yvonne like the warmth of a soft blanket and giving her some comfort. "You didn't hear what I said, did you?" His amused tone contained no malice, despite the accusatory nature of the question.

"Yes, I did," she insisted before faltering. "Well, I got the general gist—a couple...wrapped in each other's arms. I trust you."

Garvey tilted his head, nodding slightly before averting his gaze to arrange his equipment along the skirting board.

Folding up the cloth, he neatly tucked it into the corner by the window, ready for when it was needed. "Don't worry, I not gon' take too much space."

"No, it's fine," she quickly replied, embarrassed at being caught staring. "Take all the space that you need."

Her concern didn't lie with the amount of room he needed, but rather with marvelling at his level of organisation as he prepared for the project he had been hired to complete. The idea that he expected her to complain sprang to mind—the cantankerous old woman who was impossible to please.

Though only forty-one, she still considered herself old enough to be his mother—had she been the type to get pregnant as a teenager. However, she had not been wild either in her teens or at any other stage in her life. She was sensible and reliable, like a well-worn pair of comfortable shoes.

Almost laughing at the ridiculousness of her earlier thoughts, she wondered how her imagination could possibly pair her with a free-spirited young man like Garvey.

She watched the man who ignored her, his attention directed to the work that had become his priority. Feeling faintly ridiculous at doing nothing more than sitting there watching him, she shifted from the stiff pose she held as she prepared to offer him a drink, the real purpose being to get her out of the room and prevent her from appearing to be a lecherous old woman, lusting after supple young flesh. She had to say something to end the silence that had gradually become deafening.

"Do you enjoy it?" he suddenly asked, continuing to look at the wall as he stroked his pencil over the surface.

The question made Yvonne jump, coming just as she opened her mouth to ask him a question. "Enjoy what?"

"Your sex life."

Taken aback, she was unable to immediately reply, the skin on the back of her neck prickling enough to make her reach up and stroke it.

Lowering his hand, Garvey turned to her to show an expression that was even more relaxed when compared to her raised eyebrows. "I offended you?"

From the flash in his eyes, Yvonne knew he expected her to say yes, expecting her to be outraged by his insolent question. No doubt he sought a reaction, wanting confirmation that she was the prude he thought her to be.

Lifting her chin and pulling back her shoulders, she shook her head, her lips seeming to prefer remaining together over forming words.

"Course not," he instantly agreed, his smile widening to reveal a set of teeth to make a dentist proud. "You write about sex."

There was a pause as she recognised the absurdity of being uneasy because his words were true. "Exactly."

The leather creaked beneath her as she slid along the sofa, improving her view as he continued to create the drawing with which he would transform the plain white space. In mere seconds, the pencil lines began to resemble the curves only a female form could offer. Watching the beginnings of the image come to fruition caused an excitement that made Yvonne's skin tingle.

A slight curve pulled at her lips in seeing the portrait that he had designed just for her.

"How long were you married?"

Holding her breath, she flicked her gaze to his face, looking into his eyes as if they would confirm whether she had heard the question correctly.

He said nothing, displaying his confidence by steadily fixing her in his sights as he awaited a response.

"Er, did I mention I was married?" she asked, the return of her breath not making the process any less laboured as her heart pounded against her ribs.

Her back tensed at the undesirable reminder of her ex-husband, every sinew objecting to the idea of starting a conversation on the subject.

He shook his head. "Is jus' the impression I get."

Lifting her chin as she considered what impression she made, she quickly nodded as if she actually knew what he was talking about. In reality, she itched to know what he thought, making her force her tongue to the back of her teeth.

Unconsciously tapping her middle finger against her thumb, her fingers were a blur by the time the question burst from her mouth, unable to be contained. "What other impression did you get?"

Her voice sounded strained, barely recognisable to her own ear, sufficient to make her unnecessarily clear her throat.

"You haven't been with the right man yet." He spoke casually before turning back to the wall, as if he had made a casual comment about the weather.

The effect on Yvonne was far from casual, the plainly uttered sentence making her body freeze as she stared at him. Not only was she amazed that he had said it, it was equally unbelievable that he seemed in no hurry to qualify the statement.

"You can tell that just by looking at me?" she finally sputtered.

"You can tell much just by looking at someone. The face, the body and the spirit is real expressive."

Her head flicked to one side, like a nervous tic that had never bothered her before. The thought that he had been studying her since he first arrived made her nervous. Her mind drifted back over recent history. She was bemused by the idea that the youngster had enough confidence to think he could school her in the human condition. "I agree."

"You feel like you have a good imagination?"

Her brow furrowed as she sought to determine the point of the question, rather than to answer it.

"You must have a good imagination to write."

"Yes," she answered absentmindedly. "Yes, I think I do."

"So how you can't imagine the picture I drawing?"

Her smile widened, the realisation that she was being teased making her shoulders drop as her muscles relaxed. Opening her mouth to protest, she was prevented from saying anything when he beckoned her to him.

"Come, le' me show you." Remaining where he stood, Garvey held out his hand to her as if confident that she would accept it.

A few seconds passed before she followed his expectation, keeping her eyes on him and speculating about what he had planned. Putting her hand in his, she immediately felt the warm strength of it, surprised by the softness that she felt, other than a callous along the upper edge of his palm.

Allowing herself to be led as he pulled her towards him, her sense of trepidation increased as she neared him, seeing nothing but the wall of his frame. There was nowhere else for her to go but to press against his body.

For a moment, her legs trembled as if they were in danger of collapsing beneath her, despite Garvey holding her tightly.

"We standing, so you mus' imagine us lying down." As he spoke, he wrapped his arms around her, carefully and gently as if in danger of breaking her.

It was the last thing she'd expected him to do and for a moment, she went into panic mode—her body gearing up for a fight-or-flight response the rush of adrenaline demanded. Sure that the pounding of her heart was loud enough for him to hear, she tried to compensate by holding her breath. Looking up to see whether he had noticed her uncontrollable response, she found her gaze drawn to his strong jaw. She imagined her lips against it before flinching when Garvey looked down at her. "I thought you say you trus' me."

Letting her eyes fall on an interruption in the slight arch of his left eyebrow, she wondered what had caused the scar. "I do. I wouldn't have hired you otherwise."

"You lookin' nervous." He smiled, holding her gaze long enough for her to see a mischievous glint.

"I'm not."

He squeezed her harder, holding her close enough to make her release a sigh of gratification. The tension left her body as quickly and easily as a heavy breeze carrying away dry leaves.

His T-shirt didn't appear to be anything special—navy blue with the number seventy-two boldly printed on the front—but it felt softer than she'd imagined. Turning her face to one side, she let the material caress her cheek as she reached her arms around his body, relishing his warmth.

She breathed him in, the crisp, clean scent of citrus and something else she couldn't quite place.

"My arms would go here," he explained, sliding one arm across her shoulder blades while the other encircled her waist.

Her body eased as she leaned in to the clinch, relaxing in his arms. Firmly pressing her palms to his body, she gathered his shirt in a grip as she succumbed to the pleasure of the hold that felt so natural.

It was easy to picture the image he intended to paint when her body was pressed against his, picturing them in place of the anonymous couple he would use to adorn her wall.

"One of your arms would be higher," he corrected, pushing one of her arms up his back. "An' the other lower — opposite to mine."

She followed his instructions, slowly stroking her hands over his body to get them into the position he wanted, feeling each sinew respond through his clothes as he moved.

Flattening herself against his body, she tightened her grip as warmth spread through her. The sensation took over her mind, preventing her from thinking of anything but what sex with him would be like. Her mind let her imagine the weight of his body, the feel of his bare skin against hers, hot and damp with sweat, a sign of the energy he would expend.

The pounding of her heart seemed to extend throughout her body, making her feel like she was throbbing. The sensation became intense enough to make her feel as though his pelvis thumped against hers. She sprang back, loosening her hold and disentangling herself from his arms.

"Er, yes, I get it. I'll be back in a second."

As she spoke, Yvonne backed towards the door, cursing her body for betraying her during what should have been an innocent demonstration.

Rushing from the study, she didn't stop until she got into her bedroom and had closed the door behind her. Leaning back on the door, her heart pounded in her chest as she wrung her hands together as if it would get rid of the clammy sensation. *What am I doing?* Yvonne thought. *How can I possibly be thinking about sex with him? He would probably find it hilarious.*

Tilting her head back to stare at the ceiling, she berated herself for reacting so strongly to her mind's tricks. Fleeing the room just made her seem rude and slightly crazed, and the dismay that arose from imagining that he saw her that way made her reach up to run her fingers into her hair, tightly gripping a fistful.

Moving away from the door, she got as far as the centre of the room before stopping. Though she was a step away from the bed, she didn't want to sit on it—didn't know *what* she wanted. At a loss, she paced up and down over a short distance.

The knock at the door made her jump—two solid taps cutting through the silence. It was enough to make all the erratic thoughts circling in her head instantly halt. Opening her mouth, she was about to ask, *Who is it?* but stopped herself just in time, shaking her head at the ridiculousness of the question as she slowly returned to the door.

Tightly gripping the door handle, she took a deep breath before swinging it open, her preparation proving to be useless. Though she knew it was him, he still created a striking image, making her feel as she had when she first met him.

"You all right?"

"Sure, I'm fine," she replied, the pitch of her voice a little too high.

She thought about apologising for suddenly departing, for being rude enough to leave her guest alone, but she couldn't find the words.

"I have another idea," he declared, raising the camera she hadn't noticed in his hand.

"What's that for?"

"You can't see the way the body move if you can't see the body properly."

Chapter Three

"Excuse me, miss."

Turning to the man who seemed to have suddenly appeared at her shoulder, she hid her instant attraction to the dark-haired stranger with a wary glance.

"Have you ever thought about modelling?"

A wide smile held back the laughter that tickled the back of her throat, threatening to erupt from her mouth. "Is that the best you can do?"

Though entirely too savvy to fall for a line that had only one purpose, she still found it funny that he made the attempt. Besides, if he wanted to get into her underwear, he only need ask.

Sidling past her and into her bedroom, Garvey appeared not to notice the puzzled look that creased Yvonne's face.

"Y'ave a nice bedroom."

Closing the door, she turned and watched him, looking effortlessly comfortable as he regarded his surroundings while she considered the unexpected sight of him in her bedroom. "Thank you."

After looking through the window, he pressed some buttons on the camera before setting it down on the far end of the windowsill.

A close look at the small digital device confirmed to Yvonne that it was a camcorder. "Why do you have a camera with you?"

"I'm an artist," he asserted, walking towards her. "I always have a camera with me."

Garvey stood directly in front of her, forcing her to angle her face upwards in order to see him properly. His scent and his powerful physical presence alone flooded her senses, making her frame seem to tremble as if overloaded, simply by the act of holding his gaze.

"I have a still camera too — you wan' see it?"

Not needing proof of what she already believed, Yvonne responded with a slight shake of her head as her toes curled, digging into the soft pile of the rug beneath her bare feet. As surreal as the current situation was, the last thing she wanted was to take any action that would make him move from where he stood.

The offer wasn't repeated as Garvey put his arms around her as he had in her study. Somehow, it was more intense than before, immediately making a mockery of recent history. Suddenly, she could imagine nowhere else that she would rather be as she wrapped her arms around him in the same way.

His hand fell on the small of her back, a connection that could be felt against her skin as if she was naked. The heat had the same intensity as the frisson caused by the weight of his body pressed to her chest, still unable to flatten her nipples which stood proudly.

This time, she knew she had made no mistake, feeling the firm pressure of his erection pressed to her thigh. For a moment, the shock held her still, her slowly released exhale the only sound to be heard.

With her cheek pressed to his chest, she was unsure of whether the pounding she detected came from him or her. In fact, it proved difficult to even determine what it was causing the sound as it veered between a rapid thump and a deep rushing sound.

Turning her face up, Yvonne found that Garvey was ready to return her gaze, his lips parted as if silently telling her what he wanted. The same desire gripped her, her body swathed by flowing lust that continued to tighten. It bound her even as it reminded her she shouldn't want what every inch of her burned for.

The niggling doubt was beaten into submission as he leant forwards, seeming to move in slow motion as he bent to meet her lips. The slight movement was powerful enough to make her feel it before he reached her, pressurising the air between them to make the gentle touch of his mouth result in an explosion.

It reverberated through her like a shockwave, intensifying and settling at her vulva. He deepened the kiss, crushing her lips as he held her tighter.

The smouldering sensation rolled through her body as though it flowed along a stream of flammable liquid.

All her breath left her body, leaving her almost spent from a single kiss. Her grip on his body tightened as she parted her legs, pressing her body to his in the way she had wanted to ever since he walked into her house and entered her life.

He responded by thrusting his hips, giving her no option but to feel the pressure of his yearning, no less powerful with a barrier of clothing. The stiffness of his rough fly rubbed against her pelvis to stimulate her swollen clit, making the heat from his lips tepid by comparison.

Though the situation seemed unreal, like a dream that would only arrive while in the depths of slumber, it was tempered by a sense of euphoria.

Sliding her hands up his back, she inadvertently gathered his shirt. The touch of her fingers to his bare skin proved thrilling, sending heat crackling up her arms from the sparks in her fingertips.

Reaching higher, she hooked her fingers around his neck, clamping him tightly as he dipped her. The unexpected move caused a lightheaded feeling that made her laugh, the situation causing a slight hysteria.

Looking up at him helped to calm her, fierce desire evident in his expression, making real what seemed like a dream.

It took her a moment to recognise that it wasn't the reaction of her own body causing the throbbing sensation, but his. The pulsating pressure that sporadically thumped her labia resulted from his cock twitching beneath his trousers.

Holding her in the seemingly precarious position, Garvey gazed down at her, seeming to relish his new-found control. "See how else your body move."

Though she wanted to speak, to respond with a succinct sentence that would tell him how she felt, the words wouldn't come. All Yvonne could do was look back at him, wondering why he didn't appear to be as overwhelmed as she felt.

He leaned in to kiss her, and Yvonne couldn't help but giggle as she could barely recall the last time she had been treated to a gesture that made her feel so completely desired.

His lips flooded her with heat, melting her until she arched further, moulding her frame to his with the support of his solid grip.

Without warning, Garvey swept her up in his arms to easily lift her from her feet. He would only have needed to tip her backwards to leave her lying on the bed. However, he took the time to gently lay her on the sky-blue duvet of the neatly laid bed, immediately ruffling it with the weight of their bodies

She seemed to lose her breath as he climbed onto the bed with her, the beat of her heart skipping and time momentarily standing still. When it started again, time ran slowly, allowing Yvonne to enjoy the pressure of his lowered hips.

Sinewy muscles bulging in his arms, Garvey supported himself above her to dip his upper body to kiss her hungrily, seemingly unable to resist her mouth. One of his hands slid up her shirt as his mouth met hers, quickly finding her bra and surprising her with the speed with which he pulled it down to free her breasts.

Anticipating his touch, she let go of him and pressed her palms to the bed, bracing her body for his touch to her emboldened nipples. Her preparation failed to reduce the intensity of the shudder that shook her body, surprising her by the fierceness of the sensation, unlike what she had ever experienced with any other man.

Just as she began to relax, willing to surrender to him, he seemed to display some dissatisfaction by drawing back. The disappointment she felt at the removal of his hand battled with the excitement that came from experiencing his touch in the first place.

She quickly found that her fears about his opinion of her body were unfounded and was unable to refuse when he reached out to take her hand, pulling her to her feet.

"I can see your body better standing up."

A sudden self-consciousness held her frozen stiff, suffering the same anxiety she had felt the last time a man had seen her undressed. Though concerned about his reaction, she was unable to stop him, knowing she would regret not letting the situation play out. The look in his eyes encouraged her to continue despite her trepidation at the thought of being scrutinised.

His fingers deftly loosened each of the buttons her trembling fingers had struggled with that morning. She fixed her eyes on his, unable to look away as she felt him gently push the garment from her shoulders.

Pulling at the vest top beneath with his forefinger, he teasingly looked into the gap, letting his gaze drift along her cleavage. "All these layers like you trying to hide in plain sight."

Offering a sheepish smile as she shrugged her shoulders, Yvonne's self-consciousness made her wonder whether his words were merely meant to tease or whether he could read her.

She knew he had to be used to bodies much younger than hers, which caused insecurity to needle her, fighting with her body's desire to discover what he had to offer.

With the sharp swift movement he used to drag her top over her head, forcing her to raise her arms, she learnt he wasn't teasing. Searching his face, Yvonne was unable to detect even a fraction of the concern she felt at being so exposed.

In fact, all she saw was the clear look of desire that drove his actions, his dark eyes taking on a rich tone as though fire blazed beyond.

The intensity of his kiss caught her off guard, the demanding pressure of his lips making her feel like she was in a spinning room. Fortunately, a sense of balance wasn't required as he encircled her body with strong arms.

Expecting to be lifted, Yvonne was surprised when the embrace became more purposeful, gasping as the clasp of her bra suddenly loosened.

Pulling away to look at her face, Garvey appeared curious about her reaction, studying her face as if expecting protest. However, Yvonne remained silent, her lips parted in invitation as her breasts heaved with heavy breaths.

He was the one to break their eye contact, seemingly unable to keep his stare from dropping down to her bare breasts as he pulled her bra away before letting it drop to the floor.

His full bottom lip grazed her mouth on his way to her neck, leaving her wanting. He kissed her neck, swiftly moving down to trail his tongue over her breasts until he reached her nipple. He sucked the eager bud into his mouth, a gentle sensation followed by a sharp one that made her gasp as her back arched.

Fiercely grabbing her arms, he lifted her enough to press his palms to her back as if prepared to fight to prevent letting her go. It was clear to her that she wouldn't have been able to stop him even if that had been what she wanted.

Releasing his grip only slightly as he slipped downwards, Garvey surprised her by getting to his knees in front of her.

His arms encircled her waist, his fingers reaching for the zip fastening of her skirt. Yvonne recognised that her naked bosom was nothing compared to what Garvey intended. He worked quickly, apparently eager to leave her completely exposed.

She trembled as the skirt slipped over her hips, tickled by the unusual sensation of his fingertips grazing her skin. The fabric pooled at her feet and she stepped free of the garment.

The fervour increased as his hands reached up to her knickers, shimmering heat making her skin tingle as if screaming for his touch. Even as he swept his hands over her body, hovering close without touching her, she felt every movement from the heat that radiated from his palms.

It led to a sensation of her body floating, making her feel unsteady as if she stood on legs incapable of holding her up. After checking to see whether he noticed her reaction, the concern left her mind as he gripped her underwear, leaving her mind solely occupied with her imminent nakedness and his proximity to it.

Her unadorned body would be on show to a man who was undoubtedly more used to taut, lithe bodies — young women who were waxed to perfection in contrast to her triangle of downy black hair.

The caress of his fingers was as gentle as the soft brush of her cotton knickers slipping over the curves of her bottom and hips. Looking down at him, Yvonne waited for the change in his expression, something to show he was put off by what he saw. In fact, all she found was the same deep look of yearning that he'd had since he entered her bedroom.

As she stepped out of her underwear, she felt the distinct moist sensation of arousal between her thighs. With nothing to shield her, she knew he would notice her body's excited reaction, that he would detect the aroma only her body could offer.

Though she wasn't sure exactly what to expect, she felt faintly relieved that he didn't react adversely. His actions alone had fuelled and primed her body, readying her for sex, and he appeared to want nothing more than to take advantage of it.

The purpose of the slow movement of his hands travelling up from her calves seemed to be to tease both her and himself, variously feather light and firmly caressing as he continued upwards to cup her arse cheeks.

His warm breath tickled her swollen labia, washing over the middle junction of her body where her pleasure lived. He moved slowly, panning his face back and forth as if taking in her scent.

Any apprehension she had felt immediately disappeared, the sight of the contented joy he took from her body's appearance raising a smile to her lips. The image of him kneeling in front of her renewed the quivering of her body, a concentrated sensation that seemed to make pins and needles tap at her fingertips. The heat of his breath seemed powerful enough to cover her entire body, cascading down over her skin.

Though the proximity of his mouth to her sex made it a natural progression, the touch of his lips still startled her enough to make her body jolt. The unexpected caress of his soft mouth to her labia immediately made her reach out to clutch his head, weaving her fingers into his hair.

Her heart felt like it was pressed against her chest wall, pounding hard enough to make her body sway. The beat flowed down through her body, making her clit pulsate with the need for his mouth. She was unable to remember the last time she had felt a need so strongly.

He became more insistent, his grip on her bum tightening as he sought more with his tongue. The unexpected thrust of solid heat against the sensitive bud protruding between her engorged folds made her jump. His tongue was like a probe, delivering a charge of electricity that coursed through her body, demanding her compliance.

Instantly, she knew she had been lying to herself in believing that she didn't miss sex. As she looked down at him, however, she knew that he was the key to the equation. With his mouth alone, he set a raging fire that released endless sparks as it crackled through her body.

At that moment, she could remember no other man — all of them paled into insignificance when compared to Garvey. It became impossible to even recall the names of any of the few men that had been inside her as the pleasure of Garvey's skilful tongue well exceeded the satisfaction of being spread by a thick shaft. Concern that she may never get the experience again made her focus on the minor details, surrendering to every sensation and feeling them deeply, each a new experience. Previous men were easily forgotten, but it suddenly became essential that she file him in her memory.

A cool flush came with the shift of his firm grip, and sudden concern arose from the thought that something was wrong. In the few seconds it took for his hands to move around her hips, maintaining a firm pressure, to push against her inner thighs, Yvonne became racked with self-doubt. *Did I do something wrong? He must not like the taste of me.*

The pressure of his palms increased, forcing her to spread her legs wider, giving Garvey more access to the nectar he relished. He curled his body lower, attempting to fit his frame into the space created by the triangle of her parted legs in his quest for more.

A torrent of hot relief rushed through her body, mixing with the pleasure that curled out from her core, focussing her ecstasy.

The gentle teasing laps disappeared, replaced with a flesh piston that stoked the flames of fire he set. Bathing her open cleft with the breaths from deep exhales, he thrust his tongue deeply, aided in his task by a tight grip on her bum cheeks.

Yvonne rocked back on her heels, looking up at the ceiling as she became lost in a haze. It cocooned her and seeped into her body, creating a lightness that threatened to make her float away.

The state of heightened awareness took away her control, making her tightly grasp his hair as heat, light and pleasure joined together to stimulate every crevice of her body.

When she suddenly no longer had his mouth smothering her labia and sucking her clit, she felt the loss intensely. The earlier sensation was gone, leaving her with only the echoes of what had been. It turned out to be a brief pause, only long enough for Garvey to hurriedly drag his T-shirt off over his head, returning before it even hit the floor to the meal he savoured.

The wave of air that cooled her sodden cleft when his T-shirt agitated the atmosphere contrasted with the heat of his mouth, making her midriff quiver.

A bead of sweat ran down the centre of her back, synchronising with the gentle strokes of his tongue to leave her wriggling with ticklishness. Looking down, she was initially met with the sight of her own fingers lost in his thick locks, before he tilted his head up to meet her gaze.

Though she felt the loss of his mouth, teetering on the edge of a precipice, she was comforted by his smile. The wide beam was borne of gratification and lust, the look in his eyes letting her know how much he wanted her.

Each deep inhale made her breasts thrust forward, lust combined with an excitement like she had never felt made her heart beat faster. She knew that he was capable of so much more and imagining what that could be acted as a powerful stimulant.

What seemed like an age to Yvonne was, in fact, only a few seconds as Garvey went from his knees to his feet with a single acrobatic jump. Slowly unfurling his impressive frame, he offered her the opportunity to admire his lean physique, every muscle visible and inches from her fingers.

The warm brown shade of his smooth skin was like ice cream, looking delicious enough to make her want it without even knowing the flavour.

His dark, erect nipples were deeply tempting, like luscious treats she didn't have the willpower to resist. She swallowed hard as her mouth began to water.

Appearing patient, Garvey waited and watched, his abdomen gently rising and falling after his exertion.

Yvonne made the first move, raising her hand to the valley between his raised pectorals. The searing temperature of his skin surprised her, making her flinch and pull back reflexively before she giggled at her own skittishness. Returning her hand to his skin, she trailed her hand down his chest, dragging her thumb so that it hitched on his nipple.

The sweet satisfaction she got from the hum he emitted made her smile, making her want to run her tongue across the dark buds to see what further reaction she could elicit. As much as it thrilled her to know she had such influence over his body, her courage didn't extend to allow her to carry out her desire.

Instead, she watched her fingers continue downwards, caressing the unyielding muscle of his stomach until there was nowhere else for her hand to go. Letting her hand come to rest on the thick material of his waistband, she looked up to see the eager expression on his face, a picture of unconcealed bliss.

Forced to take a second glance, she could barely believe that she was the cause of his excited state. Needing to test that it was more than a fluke, she utilised the confidence it built to let her hand travel down to his tented fly. Using the back of her hand, she gently rubbed his impressive bulge with a downward stroke. The deep breath that rattled from his throat made her seek more, increasing the pressure as she drew her hand back upwards. He growled deep in his throat, the sound powerful even though it was unreleased.

Though she noticed his arm move, Yvonne's gaze remained on his face, his look of desire enough to make moisture flood her vulva, threatening to escape and flow down her thighs. She didn't notice the condom until he silently held it out to her, offering her the opportunity to carry out the task. The mere thought made her muscles contract.

She took the small square in one hand, the wrapper rustling beneath her touch, hand shaking with anticipation.

At first, the button seemed not to want to be released, forcing her to pull harder until his waistband popped open. A glance up at him confirmed she felt his gaze, his expression displaying his enjoyment of the trepidation that made her nerve endings crackle with electricity as she pulled his fly open further to drag his trousers down.

In awe of his cock the moment it sprang free, Yvonne couldn't take her eyes off the magnificent specimen. The smooth, dark flesh of his shaft was like nothing she had ever seen, like it had been sculpted as an example of what perfection should look like.

Standing proud, intermittently jumping with an eager flinch, his erection was larger than she would have imagined. Her past experiences had her mostly avoiding a man's crotch, taking up a standard position on her back to await the predictable and limited exertion of her ex-husband. However, Garvey offered something different, his rigid pole acting as a lure that drew her hand as if powerless to resist.

With a light touch, Yvonne stroked his shaft, tracing her fingers along the underside until she cupped his heavy sac. A look up at his face made her bolder, applying gentle pressure until a growl reverberated in his throat. It thrilled her, making her breath quicken as she reluctantly released him in order to rip open the condom packet.

Tentatively sliding the latex onto his ready shaft, her smooth caress continued until her fingertips teased the unruly strands of silky black hair at the hilt.

His ability to wait patiently disappeared the moment she concluded the task. It prompted him to reach for her, holding her waist to lift her as if she weighed nothing.

Yelping with surprise, Yvonne quickly got over it as she raised her legs, automatically wrapping them around his torso as her shoulders came level with his. Flattening her bosom to his chest, their skin-to-skin contact made her suddenly more aware of her rapid heartbeat.

Holding her tightly, Garvey jogged up and down to shake his trousers free, wriggling his way to nakedness as if letting her go wasn't an option. Before long, he pulled his feet free to kick his clothes away. In the few seconds the action took, he had her standing on a precipice, eagerly waiting for him to be ready to plunge off with her.

Breathing as heavily as him, Yvonne waited for his expected action, to lay her on her back. However, he surprised her by turning around to lie on his own back, her body jolting with the movement as he brought her down atop him.

Realising what he expected made her nervous, her self-consciousness reappearing as she knelt astride him, her body somehow more openly on display than before.

Being more used to the missionary position, Yvonne's poise began to fail her as she looked into his face, seeking guidance.

He flashed her a bright grin. "I like this view."

Sliding his hands up from her waist as he spoke, his easy manner boosted her confidence, making her smile back at him as he crushed her breasts beneath his palms.

The pressure of his hot thumbs against her nipples had an instant effect, like they were buttons that controlled her body. With the quick and skilled motion of his hands, stroking her skin and pinching her nipples, he demanded her actions. As his fingers trailed down her abdomen, coming to a stop at her waist, the idea that she should lift her body to guide his cock inside her became second nature.

Wrapping her fingers around the base of his firm shaft to hold it upright, she held her breath before impaling her body. The result was instantaneous, a searing heat shooting through her body to explode, leaving a trail everywhere it travelled.

With his firm grip of her hips, Garvey seemed to want to lower her gently but didn't get the chance before the explosive force of her body made him rear up to take her. The moan that punched out of his throat was like a panacea, heightening her pleasure while taking away any traces of doubt that came from being with a man so young.

Leaning back, she tightly gripped his upper thighs as she rocked her pelvis, eager to get the same reaction. The fluid motion of her body made it seem liquid, melted by the intense energy as he pounded into her body.

It quickly became apparent it would prove impossible to concentrate on his needs when her own demanded her attention so strongly. Engorged and tight, the muscles of her pussy seemed to mould to his shaft, gripping him firmly as if their bodies were a perfect fit.

With Garvey holding her waist, Yvonne rhythmically rocked her hips, the resulting sensation gradually building with regular movements.

Feeling his grip tighten as she looked down at him, she could barely believe that a man so young could easily make her sink into a state of bliss. She suddenly became timid beneath his gaze, looking at her hand as she reached for his torso, a single touch confirming that his body was on fire. In fact, his skin was hot enough to make her instantly retreat, proceeding in a more tentative manner as if lowering her body into a hot bath.

Before long, she got used to the sensation of being submerged in the heat, enabling her to hold him firmly, his muscles unyielding beneath her fingers. Spreading her thighs to take his cock deeper caused a gratifying grunt to rise from his throat, increasing Yvonne's confidence and raising her temperature to match his as if they were perfectly in sync.

The rhythmic movement of her body with his built a delicious pressure that made her lose control. Her body bucked atop his, each jerking motion making his shaft plunge deeper.

The muscles in her thighs began to burn, a sensation that climbed gradually until they screamed for mercy from the kneeling position she was unused to holding. Refusing to give them a reprieve, Yvonne leant forwards to press her palms to his nipples, their hardness like two jewels lost beneath a length of smooth satin.

His audible exhale turned her on as much as feeling his rapid heartbeat against her fingers as they strayed across his hot skin, leaving a mark in the moist sheen of sweat.

Moving her touch down to the sides of his abdomen, she braced herself against the firm sinew that bound his ribs. Her hands didn't remain there long, snatched up by Garvey who laced his fingers with hers to hold her with a grip that demonstrated the depth of his passion.

A river of fire coursed through her body, carving its own path rather than following one she could have expected, licking at hidden parts of her body that had gone forgotten for so long.

"Oh, God!"

The culmination crashed into her body, slamming her with a power she didn't expect. It stiffened her body, making her arch backwards as she lost control, releasing a high-pitched cry. Her vocal climax was powerful enough to snatch her strength, leaving her barely able to hold her body upright.

With a gratified whimper, her head tipped forwards before the rest of her body followed. He leaned up to meet her, catching her in his arms to stop her from falling.

The feeling of his damp skin was satisfying as his arms tightened around her body. The crushing embrace came with the frenzied movement of his hips, thrusting his cock hard and fast as his body rubbed against her clit until she began to tremble.

A deep growl rumbled up from his belly, a primaeval noise that in turn intensified Yvonne's arousal until she felt like her body would explode. Flattening her body to his, she wrapped her heavy arms around his neck and folded her legs behind him to cling to him. A heavy shudder seized him, shaking his body beyond his control as a juddering yell announced the arrival of his climax, thrilling her with the sensation of his shaft undulating against her walls before shrinking back as he released ribbons of cream.

Continuing to cling to him, Yvonne stroked her fingers across the moist, smooth surface of his back, feeling his heart thumping against her chest as he did the same. Relaxing in his arms, Yvonne couldn't help but think about all the time she had wasted by avoiding younger men when, all along, complete ecstasy had been awaiting her.

They continued to hold each other as Garvey lay back, moving as one while they recovered, listening to each other breathe.

"Not only do you feel good, you look good." With his face buried to her neck, his words were muffled but she still caught every word, vibrating through her body. "I love the way your body moves."

Yvonne could only giggle at the words she had never heard from any man. She would have been content to remain there in his arms but, all too soon, he rolled them onto their sides.

His face displayed the serenity that she felt, a glint in his eye revealed when he opened his eyes. He gently pressed his lips to hers as he slowly withdrew his shaft, his tongue thrusting between her lips as the slick pressure of his cock fell against her thigh. "I'm going back to work," he grinned, a glint in his eye. "You inspired me."

Though she was reluctant to let him go, Yvonne settled for watching him cross the room to collect his camera, taking no steps to hide his naked frame.

"Oh, my God!" Yvonne exclaimed. "I completely forgot about that."

Garvey unhooked the rear of the device to remove a small component, walking back to her side to place it in her hand. "You mus' look at the way your body move."

"Aren't you curious about watching it?" she asked, as he turned to walk away.

Shaking his head as he returned to her side, he leant forward to kiss her lips. "I've seen the real thing."

With that, he walked away, leaving her lying on the bed as he returned to his job.

Listening to her own breathing marring the silence, a brief moment of doubt flitted through her mind, making her wonder whether he actually meant what he'd said. However, the satisfying throb of her clit as she shifted her legs alleviated her worries.

The perfunctory sex of her past was gone, even if it was only a one-off. She curled her fingers around the proof she held in her hand, where it remained in her hot grip as she fell asleep.

Chapter Four

There was no sound, only the image on the screen of two people writhing together, their mouths open in silent moans and cries of ecstasy. Their bodies rocked in perfect rhythm, oblivious to everything apart from the passion and lust that had taken control.

"Porn?" he scoffed, a smile curving his lips. "This isn't porn."

Taking her hand, he made the glistening tone of his back her only view as he led her to a closed door of solid dark wood. He turned to her, silently compelling her to open it with an intense gaze that she found herself unable to look away from, the rich brown shade of his eyes holding her mesmerised. She found a room that contained a bed, a tripod-supported camera standing by its side. "This is erotic art."

A sudden shyness arose as Yvonne watched him through the window, time speeding up the casual stroll of his approach, causing butterflies to flutter in her stomach.

Nervously smoothing her hands over her skirt, doubting her choice of clothing, she rushed to the door as he neared it before it suddenly occurred to her that he had yet to press the bell. Taking a deep breath, she smiled to herself and sucked her lower lip into her mouth, pressing her teeth to the plump edge that Garvey had tasted. She was barely able to believe what had happened between them. It could have been like some sweet dream had it not been for the satisfying sensation of her still-swollen labia.

She remained standing by the door, waiting for him to request entry, and was surprised by the subtle knock instead of the jarring doorbell she was expecting. Though it felt like ten minutes had passed, Yvonne opened the door after a count of thirty seconds. The couple silently gazed at each other for a moment, Yvonne feeling a thrill that made her feel light enough to float away. Garvey ended the pause by offering a greeting, his dulcet tones dripping with warm seduction. "Good morning."

"Good morning," she replied, the mere sight of him making a girlish smile curve her lips. "Come in."

Before making a move to enter, he leant forwards to press a gentle kiss to her lips, instantly dispelling the nerves that were so unusual to her. "You doing okay?"

She nodded, overwhelmed by his greeting, which eased her subconscious expectation of his regret.

"Good."

After closing the door, she turned around to find him studying her with an intense gaze.

"What is it?" she asked self-consciously, briefly looking down.

"Nothing." His smile was that of a man who had been caught out, making her heart pound as she yearned for a deeper kiss. "I nearly forgot how beautiful you are."

Leaning into him, she rose up onto her toes to demand the kiss her body burned for and was rewarded for her efforts. His crisp, clean scent filled her head as his hot breath bathed her lips, the intense result belied by the tenderness of the kiss.

Her skin tingled as he stroked between her shoulder blades, slowly drifting down the middle of her back. She pressed her body to his, anticipating an embrace and eager to feel the strength of his arms. Instead, he swept his hand across the small of her back before reaching for her hand, making Yvonne react by squeezing his fingers the moment he took hold of it.

Continuing to grip her hot digits, Garvey led the way up the stairs to the room where he had been working for the previous couple of days.

Leading her to the sofa, the bowed seat having been used more in the last few days than it had in months, Garvey directed her as if the room was his own. Releasing her as she sat down, he stood back as if he needed to get the right angle from which to admire her. "You watched it?"

Looking into his eyes, she could see that he already knew the answer, betrayed by her own demeanour. "It actually gave me an idea for another story."

Garvey bobbed his head as his lips curved in a wide smile. "Good. I look forward to reading it."

She curled her body against the corner of the sofa, watching him as he prepared to continue with his work. It was difficult to take her eyes off him, observing the body that had previously given her such intense pleasure though it looked so unassuming in stone-washed blue jeans and a white T-shirt. She could recall every moment, still feeling the touch of his body despite him being several feet away.

"Actually, you're my muse for it so I really should dedicate it to you."

"Really?" he grinned, his expression shining with tickled surprise.

With a nod and a smile, she answered his question, his reaction making a warm feeling of contentment flow through her. It was enough to make it seem like his comments about her book had been made an age ago.

He stood back to consider his work up to that point, only focussing his attention for a few seconds before turning to Yvonne, as if checking she was still there. She smiled, a ready display of the warmth that flooded her chest when he looked at her.

"Last chance to change you mind," he advised, pulling paintbrushes and pots of paint from his bag.

"Why would I want to do that?"

His hair swung down over his face as he straightened up. "I want to make sure you won't have regrets?"

Her reply came instantly, not making use of a pause as he had done. "I have absolutely no regrets."

As if she had said something that required agreement, Garvey gave a gentle nod. "Good."

"What about you, do you think you may have made a mistake...with the design?"

"Not at all," he replied, shaking his head. "It's perfect."

To anyone else, the look he held her with would be nothing special but, to Yvonne, it held a strength that let her know they each knew what the other was talking about.

The sun, roused from its long lie-in, shone a few lazy rays through the window, framing Garvey with yellow light and brightening the room. She felt as if she had somehow been in control of the fireball, imagining the heat on her skin as the temperature in the room increased. In reality, there was no change and the effect was short-lived, the sun proving no match for the cloud that came to shield it. However, Yvonne continued to experience the warm sensation with every glance in Garvey's direction.

After vigorously shaking a small pot of paint, Garvey popped off the top with a screwdriver. Selecting a slim paintbrush, he dipped it into the glossy brown liquid before brushing it over a section of pencil line. A long, confident stroke resulted in a smooth application, following the curve of the female form's waist.

Yvonne found herself staring as if it was the first time she had ever seen anyone paint and she was observing some new and wondrous act. Quickly catching herself, she knew she had no real business in the study and didn't want to get caught gaping at him. She could have taken her laptop to another room, let him get on with his work, but she found it difficult to stay away.

Lacking the desire to take any action that would take her away from where she wanted to be, she sought a reason to stay.

"You never needed the video for help, did you?" she asked, the mere mention of the film making it replay in her mind.

His soft smile gave her the answer. "But I will need your help with something later on?"

The causally uttered comment immediately piqued her interest, hopeful that he would elaborate on the type of help she could provide. He didn't. Garvey turned his gaze back to the wall, nonchalantly bending over to retrieve the pot of paint, as if he failed to recognise his words could be alluring.

Her tongue suddenly felt light, floating in her mouth as she prepared to pose the question to which she wanted the answer. She had never felt so eager for information before.

By contrast, he was completely at ease, the fluidity of his limbs transferring to the lines he painted. It made her wary of revealing the neurosis that suddenly arose from her impatience, needing a distraction to prevent it.

"I bought some herbal teas," she offered, remembering the specially-made trip to the supermarket. "Do you never drink hot drinks?" she asked, concern in her voice.

"I do, just nothing with much caffeine. You don't boil bush tea?"

She chuckled, recalling the many mornings of waking to the aroma of the bush tea her mother was boiling filling the house.

"Not anymore," she replied as it occurred to her that she had never mentioned where she was from.

"You have green tea?"

Pleased by his question, Yvonne smiled and nodded, relieved that it had been one of her choices, telling herself she would start drinking it. "No sugar, I take it?"

Halting mid-stroke, Garvey held the paintbrush aloft and turned in her direction. "You read me well."

Keeping her eyes on him as she got to her feet, she let her gaze sweep over the bulging muscles protruding from beneath his sleeves. Apart from a raised line of a scar less than an inch in length, his skin was clear and taut. His apparent flawlessness extended upwards, her gaze sweeping up over his strong neck to sparkling eyes. "Do you have any vices?"

As if thinking about the question, Garvey briefly raised his eyes to the ceiling, a single line sinking into his forehead. "None that real bad for me." The glint in his eye wasn't enough to detract from the look of innocence that came with his slight smile.

"I'll be back in a minute." Hurrying from the room to hide the grin that balled her cheeks, she almost laughed to herself as she speculated about his age, illustrated with images she recalled from the video.

Making tea and the warm sensation sweeping over her body at the thought of sex with him provided a temporary distraction. As she poured freshly boiled water into two mugs, her mind returned to what help she could possibly offer him. *What if I can't do what he wants me to? What if it makes him think less of me?*

The concern remained as she padded up the stairs, the carpet soft beneath her bare feet, being careful to keep her hands steady to avoid spilling.

She barely noticed the smile and words of thanks offered by Garvey as she handed him one of the mugs, lost in her thoughts as she tried to figure out what he intended.

"Why you don't just ask?" Garvey broke the silence that had followed and reigned for several long minutes. She had resumed her position on the sofa, carefully settling into her curled-up pose with mug in hand.

"Ask what?"

"I can see in your eyes — you real eager to know what I'm talking about."

Surprised at the assertion, her muscles automatically clenched, preventing her from keeping the tell-tale expression from her face. "You can see that in my eyes?"

Tilting his head to a slight incline, he raised his eyebrows to create a look of confidence that had a hint of smugness.

"You're obviously wiser than your years."

A smile broke out on his face, wide enough to flash the shiny white of his teeth. "Thanks."

During a pause, she gazed at him closely, unable to keep her eyes on his face as they drifted down his body before returning to his face. "How old are you exactly?"

With a slow blink, his smile diminished a touch. "What does it matter?"

What did it matter? She searched for an argument she could raise to support her question. "I don't suppose it does."

The fact that he had made no attempt to discover her age didn't escape her attention, making her wonder why he didn't want to know. *He has to be curious.*

"Good. There are more important things to worry about, like you assisting me."

The teasing smile that lit his face made her sure he had intended to keep her on tenterhooks from the moment he mentioned it.

"Are you going to tell me or keep me in suspense?"

Garvey continued to trail the tip of the brush along the wall, seeming not to hear her for several long moments. Finally, laying down his paintbrush, he returned to his bag to withdraw a bottle of gold paint and a slim paintbrush, which he supported behind his ear, the tapered end protruding from beyond his hair.

"You want me to help you paint?"

"No, I want you to be the canvas."

Furrowing her brow as she held him with a pointed stare, she waited for a change to his expression that would show that he was joking. There was none.

For a moment, the only sound heard was the sound of sloshing liquid as he shook the bottle. "This is latex paint, perfectly safe to paint skin with."

"Latex?"

"It's like a second skin, you can just peel it off when it dries."

"What are you talking about?" she asked, setting down her mug as disbelief made her grip too tight, her fingers straining. "What do you mean? Paint me naked?"

Twisting his lips, Garvey couldn't hide the fact that he found her reaction funny. "That's the idea. What? You shy?"

Though she couldn't imagine how it was possible, a sudden coyness crept over her, making her neck prickle as she looked down at the steam curling from her mug. The day before she had been far from introverted, in fact, she had the film to prove it. The memory of how she had been glued to the screen emboldened her. The recollection of their bodies moving as one was enough to make her also recall the fire that resulted from being so bold.

"No, I'm not."

Appearing to be attempting to hide his appreciative smile, he inclined his head forwards as he moved towards her. As he sat next to her, he held out the bottle to allow her to examine it.

She scanned the label, concentrating on ensuring that she left no sign of her hot hands on the new, unopened bottle, and not reading a word.

The warm touch of his hand falling across her inner elbow was a reassurance, making her less concerned about what his idea entailed. His gentle caress continued up her arm, calming her mind further as he pushed up her sleeve.

Hitching the material up on her shoulder, Garvey lowered his head to press his lips to the exposed curve at the top of her arm. Watching the man she was so taken by, she saw it coming, but knowing what to expect failed to prevent the result. The gentle kiss caused a shimmering heat to rise from her pelvis, relaxing every muscle of her body until they felt as though they turned to liquid. His silent lips told her that she would carry out his request, and refusal didn't enter her mind.

Simply being close to him made her body tremble powerfully enough to make her pelvis feel like it was rocking, leading to her entire body quivering. She wondered if he could feel her body moving. Looking for a sign of his recognition, his eyes only showed his feelings for her, which was more than enough for Yvonne.

Stroking his thumb across her inner arm, Garvey held her gaze as he slowly raised his head. "I'll do a skin test here."

"Why?"

"It's safe, but I want to check for a reaction, make sure you're not allergic."

Sure that his idea had only come about to get her naked, she almost laughed at the contrast of his concern.

A tempting smile remained on his lips as he raised his eyebrows, silently questioning her response.

"Okay."

His smile widened before he took the bottle from her, slipping it from her hand before twisting off the top, the seal cracking beneath his single twist. The removal of his hand came with the touch of his thigh, shifting so that it pressed against hers as if replacing one type of contact with another. Sliding the paintbrush from behind his ear, he dipped it into the neck of the bottle and withdrew it gleaming wet with gold paint.

Handing her the bottle, he gently grasped her free arm, leaning forwards to manipulate her position to access the inside of her arm. After painting an outline of an inch square, he filled it in to create a solid block of gold against the deep brown of her skin.

Yvonne tried not to flinch at the slight tickle of the wet strands moving over her skin. The cool sensation intensified when he blew on her arm, the temperature of his breath warm on her bare skin and changing as it flowed over the paint-covered section.

"It'll dry in a couple minutes."

Taking the bottle back from her, Garvey stood, the sofa creaking with his movement as if complaining about his departure.

Remaining seated, Yvonne briefly looked at the arm she held in the air, away from her body. Though the position felt awkward, the last thing she wanted to do was smudge the test application. Her gaze switched to Garvey, watching as tightened the lid back onto the paint bottle before withdrawing some plastic beakers from his bag.

"You wanna put the heating on?" Leaving his tools by his bag, he stood and looked in her direction. "In case you get cold."

"I don't think I'll need it."

Accepting her words with a toss of his head, he turned to walk to the window. Watching the flowing movement of his body as he twisted the rod to close the blinds, cocooning them further, she recalled how his body had moved the day before. The sudden rush of heat through her body made her gasp and draw in her stomach, as if bracing herself for the climax that previously had shaken her body.

She knew that no external heating would be necessary.

"What's wrong?"

"Erm, I think it's dry," she quickly replied, shrinking back as he returned to her, sure that he would feel the heat radiating from her body.

Looking at her arm, she was pleased to see that at the edges the paint looked like it was stuck to her skin rather than sitting atop it, hoping it stopped her from being a liar.

Garvey gently clasped her forearm as he sat next to her, the heat intense despite his light touch, and angled her arm to get access. Lightly tapping the pad of his forefinger against the square of paint, the action had no effect other than to let Yvonne feel the short beat.

"Good. You can peel it off now."

With the instruction, he released her, taking away the touch that she suddenly realised she craved. Raising her arm higher, she looked into his eyes. "I don't know how."

Bending over her, Garvey's hair swung forwards, partially obscuring his face as he concentrated on peeling off the paint without hurting her. After finding his not-long-enough nails unsatisfactory, he used his thumb to rub the paint off her skin in a single piece.

After displaying the small strip of latex on his palm, Garvey stroked the section of arm from which the paint had been removed.

Watching his hand move over her skin, the tone of his brown skin a little lighter than hers, she couldn't help but consider how good they looked together. Her arm was unchanged, impossible to know where the paint had been.

"You're not allergic," he smiled, satisfied and slightly cocky.

Taking her hand, he straightened up and pulled her to her feet. For a moment, he remained silent, looking at her as if he was preparing to say something.

Tilting her face upwards, she waited patiently for words to come from the lips she knew capable of providing pure bliss. However, she found that she had read him wrong when he leant forwards to bring his lips level with her ear, his fingers at her chin.

"You can start getting undressed, while I get some water for the brushes."

Picking up one of the plastic cups, he shot a quick glance in her direction before leaving the room, a smile lighting his face.

Yvonne remained unmoving as she listened to his footfalls fade towards the bathroom, sure that his cheeky expression was a sign that he recognised and enjoyed her nerves.

Looking down at her soon-to-be-naked body, she noticed a slight twitch to her left hand, gripping it with the right hand when she saw it happen again. It was ridiculous—she knew it was—because he had seen her before, but this knowledge didn't stop the spasm from moving to her leg and making it tremble.

Successfully shaking it into submission, the feeling of imminent exposure couldn't be cast off so easily. She put it down to the difference in circumstances, as the day before she had been caught up in the moment—almost intoxicated, like she wasn't herself. This was different— she was sober and the nerves caused by needing to reveal herself in the near future weighed heavily.

"You not ready yet?" There was no surprise in his tone, as if he'd returned to an expected scene.

Remaining tight-lipped, she looked at him through narrowed eyes, trying to figure out whether he was judging her as much as she was herself.

Setting down the water, Garvey took a folded-up sheet from his bag. Saying nothing as he gripped the edges to flick it in the air, his contented expression was momentarily hidden from Yvonne as the clean white fabric floated through the air to settle on the floor.

With nothing else to occupy her attention, Yvonne considered his level of organisation. "Do you always walk around with latex paint?"

Knowing that he would look at her to answer the question, she felt a sense of security from hiding her face as she pulled her shirt over her head, even while she exposed her body. Besides, she was sure he would make a comment about her reluctance to undress otherwise, and she didn't want to give him the satisfaction of thinking her cowardly.

With the shirt free from her face, she could looked into his eyes as she patted her hair. He was now kneeling on the floor as he patiently waited to offer a reply. "No, I don't."

There was no hesitation in his voice. He steadily held her gaze, waiting for her reaction. The three simple words caused a feeling of calm to wash over her, a smile pulling at her lips as the all-consuming nerves quietly departed. "How did you know I would agree?"

The question hung in the air as she reached around her back to undo the button fastening her skirt. The even rasp of the zip being smoothly slid down was the only sound before the quiet rustle of her wriggling out of the skirt. Her critical gaze studied her skin as more of her legs were revealed, and she wondered how much of her body he intended to paint.

Only when the skirt pooled at her feet and she returned his gaze did Garvey offer a response. "I must be psychic."

Standing only in her underwear didn't prevent the smile which rose to her face. She was comfortable enough to withstand the scrutiny she'd expected. "Do I need to put anything on my skin first?"

Her confidence grew enough to make the question a calculated one, ensuring that he would be looking at her when she unhooked her bra. His eyes remained on her as she slipped the straps from her shoulders, letting the garment drop to reveal her breasts. The moment they were free, her nipples immediately swelled as though they had been waiting for the opportunity to get some attention.

"You don't need anything at all."

Tickled by the sight of him failing in his attempt to keep his eyes on her face, she maintained a smile to keep from releasing the giggle that rose in her throat.

He patted the sheet-covered floor in front of him, all that was needed to beckon her.

Brazenly, she slid her thumb into the waistband of her last shield against nakedness, pulling it away from her body. "Don't I need to take these off?"

"Not yet."

Moving slowly, she walked across to where he sat, remaining standing long enough to watch his gaze drift down her body. She was close enough to feel the warmth of his breath tickling her skin, making her muscles taut before they slackened and turned to jelly.

Her knickers seemed to become tight as she lowered herself to the floor, mirroring his kneeling pose.

Reaching across, he shook the bottle again before pouring a little into the empty plastic cup. "You comfortable?"

"Perfectly."

Watching him prepare the paint to apply to her skin, Yvonne was suddenly very aware of the silence. Background music would have been an easy way to solve the problem, but she wasn't inclined to relinquish her position. Doing anything that would disrupt the situation was out of the question.

At that moment, she felt like they were the only two people in the world.

Her tongue remained still while her eyes followed him. Talking seemed unnecessary, an idea that Garvey also appeared to share.

Yvonne instead used the opportunity to study him, watching the concentration on his face as he stirred the paint. His expression took on a sudden lightness that told her he was satisfied, making him look even younger than his years.

Conscious of her status as his canvas, wanting to become his art, she became very aware of every sensation that affected her body, inside and out. The more she tried to keep her body still, the heavier her breathing became, deep breaths that shifted her abdomen. In her desire to do the best for him, she searched for a sign that he was displeased with any of her actions. She found none.

Only raising his head slightly, he met her eyes through thick eyelashes, offering a look that made her heart swell and her body relax.

Holding her hands neatly folded together in her lap, she remained still as he lifted the brush to her right shoulder. The tickling feeling she expected didn't arrive, only a strange coolness that came with the unaccustomed moisture there.

Watching his eyes flick to her face from her shoulder, she wondered whether he was concerned about her well-being, sure that she saw a look of concern. However, she opted to say nothing as he went back to concentrating on his artwork and his face relaxed.

With a slim brush, Garvey painted lines horizontally across her shoulder, stroking it towards her breast. Though his contented expression didn't change, she couldn't take her eyes off him.

His gaze was intently trained on the trails of paint he left on her skin, making her wonder what he would see when he did look to her face. A quick smile lifted her lips as the answer came to mind—she knew that he would see adoration.

The continuous sensation of coolness that came when he applied the loaded brush to her skin quickly dissipated, her body temperature quickly taking care of drying the paint. Once it matched the heat of her body, it felt like her skin was bare.

Rather than the exposure she feared, being near-naked in front of him made her feel open. The strange feeling that resulted from a never-before-considered situation became a comfort, making her smile as she watched him work.

As he smoothly swept the brush lower, his breathing became audible, deep and even despite no external change to his demeanour.

"Are you okay?"

A look came over his face as though the question surprised him, followed by a quick nod. "Just hot."

Depositing the paintbrush in the cup of water, he leant back as he crossed his arms over his abdomen to grip the hem of his T-shirt. Pulling it up to slowly reveal his taut body, she couldn't help but wonder whether his slow movements were for her benefit. She became sure they were when she saw the look in his eyes after the shirt was clear, dragging his dreadlocks to the side before he left the T-shirt in a crumpled heap.

Though he tried to hide it, she was sure that she could see his hunger, the urge that built for her. It sent a frisson of excitement through her, making her already erect nipples feel full and ripe.

Relishing her improved view, Yvonne let her gaze drift slowly down his torso, the type of which she had only ever seen on men in magazines and on billboards. Her gaze alighted on his crotch, thrilled at the movement she was sure she saw.

Raising her gaze, the mischievous look she found glinting in his eye sent a frisson through her. Suddenly, a number of thoughts streamed through her mind, of her ex-husband, her staid life and the predictable sex she had endured. As if attempting to physically shake the thoughts away, her body jerked. It succeeded in clearing her mind, replaced by an urge to stroke her fingers down his firm abdomen, feeling a sudden desire to rake her nails across his skin to see how he would react.

The sensations within her seemed delayed from the previous day, making her curse for body for being surprised by his advances, not acting in the way that she should have.

He leant back, highlighting the muscles across his torso as he pulled his body tight. Pursing his lips as he gazed at her shoulder, the look was intense enough to prompt Yvonne to twist her neck in an attempt to see what he saw.

"I need you to lie down."

Moving aside, Garvey gave offered her the space to carry out the softly spoken command, which she promptly did. Supporting her weight on one arm, she leaned to the side to unfurl her legs from beneath her body. Stretching them out, she barely felt the twinges that jabbed at her thighs, complaining of being constricted.

Instead, she recalled the last time she had lain in front of him, arching her back as she shuffled forwards, feeling the warmth he left behind as she took over his space.

The soft sheet slid beneath her, quickly warmed by the heat from her body as she settled into a supine pose.

Garvey responded the moment she lay still, leaning over her and supporting his body on arms strapped with sinew. Crawling over her body, he planted one of his knees between her legs while the other remained at her side, hovering over her as if his intentions didn't involve paint.

Sinking his body lower, his muscles bulged as he moved his frame down, holding her gaze as he appeared to seek a kiss.

Though their bodies weren't touching, her body reacted as though they were, an intense flash making her body jolt, her parted legs closing around his thigh.

Despite the obvious hiatus in the latex paint application, the couple remained silent, satisfied with reading each other through their eyes alone. His eyes only briefly left hers to follow his hand as it moved, setting her body alight with the gentle caress of his fingers.

The quiver caused by his wide hand slowly moving between her breasts initially seemed minor, but grew to manifest itself deeper. Her insides twisted as his fingers continued a route down the centre of her body, making her back lift off the floor, pushing her eager breasts higher.

Pressing her palms to the floor, she braced herself, gripping the sheet in tight fists.

His touch made her skin crackle with electricity that shook her core, making her vulva pulsate with yearning, warm moisture trickling along the cleft between her cheeks.

"I gon' stop here." He pressed his palm to her waist, holding his fingers in place before circling his thumb around to squeeze her flesh.

"So I didn't need to take off my skirt?"

Meeting her gaze after slowly sweeping up her body, Garvey offered a brazen smile. It didn't hide the desire in his eyes, making her wonder what she had been worried about in the first place. "You coulda got paint on it."

Yvonne laughed, her shaking breasts attracting Garvey's gaze.

Though he seemed reluctant, he turned back to the paint, selecting a thicker paintbrush to dip into it. His chest swelled with the deep breath he took as he leaned over her vulnerable frame, resuming what he had started.

"Are you still hot?" She successfully managed to make the loaded question sound innocent, the mere sight of him intensifying her yearning and tempting her into asking him to abandon the paintbrush.

A knowing smile split his lips, displaying a perfect row of white teeth. "Do I look hot?"

The chance to respond was lost as the bristles of the brush smoothly continued down her body, soon gently caressing her breast. Only the slightest nudge to her swollen nipple made her gasp, a rush of heat coursing through her body from the sensitive tip. Somehow, the paint seemed colder there than it had on any other part of her skin, taking her breath away.

Her back arched, her body suddenly only supported by her shoulders, bottom and toes. The minor touch fuelled her need, stimulating the depths of her core with that single stroke of the paint-soaked tip.

Sinking back down to the sheet, she quivered, though she was far from cold.

Seeming to relish the reaction, Garvey drew his brush back in the other direction, his feather-light touch serving to intensify the sensation enough to make her offer a breathy moan.

Letting the paintbrush drop from his fingers, Garvey appeared to believe his hands would be better utilised caressing her body. Raising his head to look down at her, he smoothly stroked up the curves of her waist and over her stomach, tracing a symmetrical pattern up the centre of her body.

After the ticklishness of his fingers caressing the cleft between her breasts, he countered the feeling with a firm, circular movement massaging her neck.

"I *am* still hot," he admitted, looking at her from beneath eyelids heavy with arousal. "But you only have yourself to blame."

Smiling broadly, Yvonne felt a giggle bubbling in her chest as she awaited his justification. Rather than offer one, he tilted his head to press his mouth to her neck, his muffled words deep enough to reverberate through her body, seeming to make her body vibrate.

"I'm to blame?" she laughed.

He kissed his way downwards, carving a route down her décolletage to her paint-free nipple, smothering the swollen tip with the heat of his mouth. Sure he had heard her, Yvonne smiled at the idea of him being too drawn to her body to offer a reply.

With her eyes closed, she relished the caress of his lips and tongue, alternating between gentle and forceful to heighten the warm sensation that tickled her nerve endings. Every inch of her skin felt the pleasure offered to just one small section, her body feeling more alive than it had in a long time.

Only when she was suddenly left missing his mouth did she deign to speak again. "You were the one who wanted to paint me."

Opening her eyes, she found that the rustling sound was the result of him loosening his trousers to let them drop to the floor, quickly followed by his underwear.

"You didn't refuse," he contended with a teasing smile.

The question failed to distract her from marvelling at his body, preventing her from offering a reply. She was vaguely aware of an argument that she could make which would continue the debate, but she had no inclination with him standing naked in front of her.

His was a body that looked like it had been sculpted naturally, rather than forced by the contraptions housed in a gym. The rich brown of his skin seemed to enhance his definition, displaying the bundles of smooth sinew in a lean body that was regularly used.

Kicking his clothes aside, he appeared sure of himself, unconcerned about whether or not he was being watched and admired.

For a moment, as he drew his eyes up her body to meet her gaze, she imagined how many other women had admired him in the same way, wondering what number had lain there looking up at him to await the ecstasy of his body. She reasoned it could be the source of his confidence, enabling him to stand naked in the middle of her study without any qualms.

The thoughts rushed through her mind, flashing through her consciousness as she quickly concluded she didn't care.

Comfortable on a floor she had never lain on before, paint drying on her skin, Yvonne was unconcerned about anything but the reaction of her own body and the need to satisfy its burning craving.

What she didn't know failed to worry her — he was here with her now. The man who she was in awe of wanted her, the mere sight of him sufficient to cause a deep pulse to affect her clit.

Watching him casually toss back his heavy hair made her body writhe in anticipation of the gratification he would offer, urgently needing the delicious pressure that only his solid form could provide.

As he folded his body to return to his knees, a trickle of warm moisture dribbled from her pussy to stream along the cleft between her cheeks. She was sure he would detect her scent as he leant forwards, sliding his palms up her legs as if needing to feel the way to his destination.

The hunger on his face was evident as she felt his fingertips graze her skin, the combination making her hope he did sense her arousal as he took hold of her underwear.

Looking at her as he removed her last item of clothing, the flash of Garvey's eyes from beneath heavy lids filled her with a sensation that made her entire being feel light enough to float away. It persisted as she lifted her lower body sufficiently to enable him to slip the material over the curve of her bum and down the length of her legs.

Their gazes never left each other as he discarded the item of clothing atop his own, making her feel desired with only the power of a lingering look. Alongside every tender touch, he silently conveyed how much he wanted her, feeling adoration through each action.

With his hands leading the way up her body, his slow movements seemed out of place when contrasted with the firm pressure of his urgent kiss.

Spreading her legs to accommodate him, she enclosed his waist with her arms, firmly caressing his muscles as she stroked up his back. The confidence that built as she explored every nuance of his taut back felt alien, something she would never do, but she delighted in it, savouring every moment and every inch of his smooth skin.

Holding him in a tight embrace as their passionate kiss continued, Yvonne couldn't hear the words he attempted to utter. Whatever they were, they were not important enough to make his lips leave hers. He caused the words to be lost in her mouth, leaving her only able to hear the word *taste* and nothing else.

Her heart thudded against her ribs, the single word enough to heighten the burn from the skin-to-skin connection despite the context remaining unknown. Though she was curious to know what he'd said, her body turned to liquid and prevented her from thinking straight.

With a sudden urgency, he reached down to force his hand between their bodies rather than making the movement necessary to create a gap. His fingers quickly found her sticky slit, the pads of his digits firmly stroking between her folds to find her pleasure.

Pulling away from the kiss, Garvey watched her, his eyes dancing about eagerly as he studied her face. The pressure on her sensitive bud parted her lips in a breathy cry as her body arched.

A sound like a muffled growl turned into deep sigh, a gratifying sound that prompted Yvonne to look back to his face. He successfully conveyed an expression of serene delight, despite his shining eyes.

His expression drew Yvonne's hands, making her reach up to his face, stroking her fingers along his jaw as if studying the contours of his face. Her tender touch didn't last, the desire building inside her to make her clasp him more firmly.

Looking into his eyes told her what she needed to know – she could see his desire and hoped he could see hers. As her gaze drifted to his mouth, she let her hands slip to his neck, only briefly releasing him from her forceful grip.

Desperate for the touch of his lips to hers, she inadvertently clawed at him, her body taking over to demonstrate her craving. She was sure that he recognised her need, watching her face like he was admiring a painting, but he chose to ignore it for now. Instead, a slight curve of his lips came as he rammed two fingers deep between her walls, watching her face as he set her body alight with only his dexterous digits.

The pressure created by his actions quickly built within her, swiftly rising higher until it burst from her mouth in a breathy high-pitched yell.

Surprised by the powerful reaction Garvey could coax from her body, Yvonne gazed at his face as she wondered if he was aware of his sexual prowess. She could only offer an open-mouthed grin as she decided he had to know – he knew her body and how to get what he wanted from it.

What felt like a ball of energy exploded inside her, giving her the strength to pull her body closer to his, tightly coiling her arm around his neck. Aiming to close the gap between his lips and hers, she pushed down against her toes for leverage, drawing upon everything within her to lift her body higher.

Doing nothing to aid or hinder her, Garvey continued to stroke her walls, plunging as deep as the rest of his hand would allow.

Clamped to his chest, Yvonne felt the quickening pace of his heart as his breath blasted her neck. The slow, deliberate motion of his fingers affected more than the engorged walls he connected with. The sensation of being caressed extended to her entire body, flame rolling through her insides.

Gripping him tightly, she prepared for the slow burn to gradually build, sure that it was impossible for him to take her body further, her lungs struggling to keep up with the breaths her body needed.

Only a few seconds passed before Yvonne realised that Garvey had other ideas. The strength of his hand increased as he crooked his fingers, firmly pressing his thumb to her clit. Somehow, he seemed to reach her core.

"Oh, God," she breathed, barely audible after a sharp intake of breath.

Garvey's hum vibrated his chest, making the sound echo through her. "I love that sound."

The ferocity of the fire that coursed through her left her unable to offer a substantial reply. Her trembling body began to fail her, sapping her strength as her hot skin slid against his on her way back to the floor.

Admitting defeat as her calf muscles screamed in protest, Yvonne laid beneath him, under the control of his fingers. Her body rolled in a wave, lifting her hips and arching her back as Garvey circled his thumb against her engorged bud. The strength of the hunger she felt didn't surprise her—the deep desire she had for him had been gradually building until she felt positively voracious.

Her heart swelled, filling with her craving for him and surging in her chest until she felt ready to burst. His probing fingers teased her, bringing her to the point where he wanted her to be...on the edge of ecstasy.

In her mind, she begged, desperate for him to satisfy her need, but her throat could only produce intermittent high-pitched notes.

"I love watching you," he whispered, seemingly to himself. "You're so beautiful."

Trembling beneath his touch, compliments ran through her mind but she could voice none of them. Under his control, she found that she was only able to grasp the sheet beneath her, tightly twisting it in her fists as her legs stiffened.

The pressure of the weight of his frame was a worthy replacement to his fingers, giving her the skin-to-skin contact she craved as he squashed her breasts. The heat of his body increased her temperature, enhancing the sensation of his rigid shaft pressing against her, felt through her whole body though aligned with her thigh.

Pushing his hips against her, he forced his shaft harder to her skin in what she thought was a boastful act, demonstrating the length and strength he possessed.

She sighed gratefully, tightening her embrace by sliding her hands up his back, letting her fingers caress the shapes moulded by his muscle. Pressed beneath his hard body, he seemed to want to leave an imprint on her body, making her want to feel more of him.

The eager twitch of his heavy shaft against her engorged labia encouraged her need, strong enough to raise her arm to catch his when he reached for his trouser pocket.

"Please." Her voice was so hoarse and swollen with lust that it sounded like someone else.

Lifting his face from where it was buried against her neck, Garvey met her eyes, his brows curved questioningly.

"I want to feel you." Just saying the words excited her, the thrill of spontaneity felt more keenly for being so rare.

Smiling his agreement, he curved his body to create a gap large enough to accommodate his arm. As he reached between their bodies, his weight supported on one arm, he exposed her warm body to the cool air. Looking up at him, Yvonne held her breath as she awaited her desire, her mind treating her to the recollection of how it felt to be spread by his thick flesh.

The memory couldn't compare to the reality as he guided his head to her entrance, teasingly prodding her with firm thrusts.

"Oh God, please."

Giving in to her plea, Garvey watched her face as he slowly sank his shaft deep.

Though no one had disputed it, she felt vindicated by the instant explosion that resulted from his entry.

Her body bucked beneath him, arching high enough to reach the point where he held his upper body aloft. Sinking back down to rest on her back, she looked up at him—to the fire simmering in his eyes, gradually growing as she watched.

Garvey supported himself above her with ease, his biceps taut and his shoulders bulging with the effort. Holding his upper body still, he moved only his hips to deliver long strokes of his shaft.

His locks hung down, obscuring his face until she felt the need to reach up, holding them back to study him.

She ran her feet up and down the back of his legs, tickling her arches on the wiry hairs. The combination of the feeling to her sensitive feet and the pressure of his swollen flesh against her walls made her smile, turning to a laugh as she saw the white of his teeth beyond his full lips.

Rocking her body in time with the motion of his, she felt satisfaction akin to slowly lowering her body into a warm body of water. The heat enclosed her, caressing every inch of her skin as the sensual comfort of his body controlled hers.

A pulse in his neck throbbed frantically, letting her imagine it to be his heartbeat as she wrapped her legs around him, pressing her heels to his butt cheeks.

The sight of him filled her with desire, leaving her unable to take her eyes off him, silently willing him to kiss her.

The muscles in his shoulders twitched as he complied with her desire, brushing her face with dreads that smelt of a clean scent she couldn't place.

Keeping his back arched, Garvey appeared to be holding back, preventing his weight from falling onto her. However, Yvonne had no such qualms and reached beneath his arms, gripping his back to drag him down atop her, immediately gratified by his mass pinning her to the floor.

Completely at his mercy, Yvonne felt like she was immersed in him, creating a deep connection from which she didn't want to break away. Her faculties were no longer required as she gave her body and mind to him, accepting that he was in control, determined to take him with her.

It was as if the couple were on a journey together, oblivious to anyone and everything as they wrapped around each other.

Feeling as if she was floating despite the weight of his frame, Yvonne's laboured and heavy breathing flooded his neck as she clung to him, her eyes closed as she relished every movement of his hips.

Beneath her, the sheet slid about on the smooth surface of the wood floor, every movement causing her to shift.

Soon, she found it impossible to keep her legs around his body, needing to plant them on the floor to brace herself for the wave building inside her. Her body curved so that her entire back pressed against the floor, the natural arch forced away like she was attempting a yoga stretch. The move lifted her pelvis, tilting it and pushing towards him as if offering more than she already had.

The sheet slipped beneath her feet, making her toes curl and grip the material in a vain attempt to steady herself. She compensated for her legs by gripping him more tightly, causing her arms to slip across his sweat-slicked back before she dug her fingers into his shoulders.

Without breaking pace, Garvey lifted his upper body with his arms firmly planted either side of her head, giving him the opportunity to cast his admiring gaze at her. She quickly recognised that his intention was not merely to look at her, but also to create a space between them sufficient to fit his arm.

Maintaining his position on one arm, sinews twitching beneath his gleaming skin like rope suddenly being pulled taut, the fingers of his other hand tickled her stomach on his way to his destination, making her back arch. Forcing his hand between their sweat-coated skin, his thumb found her raging bundle of nerve endings, applying a delicious pressure that instantly pounded her body like an explosion.

Crying out with an intensity that left no air in her body, she stiffened as her body arched, stretching as the intensity he offered took control. The rapid movement of his finger made it feel like it was vibrating, skilfully working her body into a frenzy with the force he applied to her cream-slicked clit.

Arching her body until the top of her head rested against the floor, Yvonne braced her palms against the floor, her eyes tightly screwed shut as she was carried away on a wave of ecstasy.

The low growl that came moments later surprised her, piercing through the sound of her own heavy breathing. Watching his face as she rolled her back to the floor, Yvonne's recovery was put on hold as stimulation rose in her at the look of pained pleasure creasing his face. Reaching up, she gripped his arse, her fingers digging harder as she felt his muscles clench and become firm beneath her touch. The rumbling sound from his throat turned into a roar, his body stiffening as an orgasm slammed into him, his hair flying through the air as he threw his head back.

With a deep exhale, Garvey withdrew and lowered his frame to cover hers, his skin hot and damp as he let the full extent of his weight rest against her.

Still, he wasn't heavy enough to prevent to rise and fall of her breasts as blissful waves continued to ripple through her body. Near breathless and pinned beneath him, Yvonne felt the sort of pure joy she hadn't felt in an age. She began to wonder what else she could have missed out on as a result of her inability to be spontaneous.

Though she would have liked him to remain where he was, Yvonne said nothing when Garvey began to stir almost right away.

Slipping off her body, Garvey lay on his side, moulded against her, his leg crossed over hers and his head resting against her shoulder.

Shuffling closer still, Garvey crossed his arm over her body to hook his fingers over the side of her waist.

As the light-headed feeling began to fade, Yvonne opened her eyes to glance at him, the weight of his arm satisfying against her sticky skin. For a moment, she was hypnotised by the swift rise and fall of his limb, caused by her own deep breaths manipulating her torso. Finally dragging her gaze away, she noted the paint left puckered and smudged, easily forgettable had she not looked down. The imprint of his body made her gold second skin matte, while her surrounding skin glistened with sweat.

"You spoilt my paint," she gently scolded, dipping her gaze to fall along her body.

A lazy smile parted his full lips before he dipped his head, the soft stroke of his locks feeling intense brushing against her sensitised skin as he kissed her collarbone. "Nothing on you could spoil."

Her gratitude tripled from what it would have been for a normal compliment, knowing that she must present a sweaty, wrung out mess at that moment. "Thank you."

"Besides, if you passing blame, you must look to yourself," he stated, his matter of fact tone increasing her disbelief.

"Me?" The pitch of her voice rose, utilising the final dregs of energy in her body. "What did I do?"

Stroking his chin along her jaw, Garvey responded by kissing her hungrily, plunging his tongue between her lips the moment his pair met hers with renewed zeal. "The flesh is weak," he whispered after taking her to complete breathlessness, his mouth moving against hers. "You can't look so sexy and expect me to resist. I'm only a man."

With her breasts rising and falling, Yvonne silently held his gaze, though in her mind she felt like cheering. The celebratory yell could have been for herself for having chosen him and brought him into her life, but it also could have been for him for making such a change once he was there. Quickly recognising that her addled mind could come to no conclusion, she put it aside to bask in the delight created by the combination of his words and his presence, wondering if he knew what he was doing to her.

Stroking his fingers across her forehead, Garvey watched their route as he caught some errant strands of her hair, his body giving a sudden, heavy shudder. His gaze returned to hers as he brushed them back, using a delicate touch that belied the strength of his large hands. "I could paint a whole outfit on you."

Yvonne laughed hoarsely, her breasts bouncing as her body trembled with mirth. "I'm sure that would go down well at the supermarket."

Tracing his fingers along her hairline, Garvey chuckled as he continued on a downward course until he reached her neck, curling his palm around one side to stroke her jaw with his thumb. "No, not the supermarket. You could wear just paint to a club."

Turning her head, she looked at him from the corner of her eye. "A club?"

She giggled as he clambered over her body, reaching for his bag from which he withdrew his Smartphone

Offering no reply, instead Garvey tapped buttons on the device. In seconds, he offered it to her after flipping it around to display the screen to her gaze.

Looking closely, she saw the miniature images of the webpage of a company that appeared to be called *Illicit Liaisons*. They had illustrated the events they held with a picture of a man and woman who looked like they had walked out of a period drama, albeit a scandalous one. Hiding their identity with masks, the couple looked poised for a clinch, the woman holding up the full skirt of her dress, displaying a single bare leg up to the curve of her bum.

Yvonne held the handset out to him. "Maybe the type of club that you young people go to."

A look of bemusement passed across his face like a fleeting shadow, serenity returning as he tapped his thumb on the screen before passing it back.

The homepage had been replaced by one that comprised a list of rules — *don't assume that your participation is wanted, no means no, only couples and single women can attend, no entry without tickets, no entry after eleven o'clock...* Yvonne only needed to skim a few of them before getting the general idea. "Have you been before?"

"No," he replied plainly. "A friend of mine told me about it."

"Yes, a friend of your age," Yvonne declared definitively. "No doubt like all the people that attend these things."

She got only a dismissive snort in reply as he took the phone back, scrolling to yet a different page before returning it to her hand.

Already, her life had changed beyond all recognition since he arrived, but Yvonne couldn't help but think this was a step more than she could handle. She watched the gallery of images that changed every few seconds, noting that the company seemed to put on a number of different events, variously seeing patrons in fancy dress and beachwear. "Are you serious?"

His eyes remained steadily trained on her, letting her know the answer without the need for words.

Looking back at the screen, Yvonne breathed deeply, attempting to disperse the nerves that rose in her chest like a dense, spreading fog. "I'm not sure," she admitted, her voice faltering.

Tossing his locks to one side, Garvey lay his head against her painted breast like he was prepared to drop the subject. "How are you going to know if you like it if you don't try?" Against her chest, his voice reverberated through her like a tempo being pounded on a bass drum.

He stirred a sense of adventure in her that she thought she had given up years before. Turning her head to continue looking at the small screen, she accepted that what should be a ridiculous, instantly rejected suggestion somehow didn't sound that way when it came from Garvey.

Filing the web address to memory, Yvonne placed the handset on the floor by her side, making a mental note to explore the website more fully later on. "Okay, let me think about it."

Remaining snuggled against her, Garvey acknowledged her with a slight nod of his head.

Relief flowed through her as silence reigned, enabling her to enjoy the traces of pleasure that continued to flow through her, her pussy pulsing in time with the rise and fall of his head on her chest.

"Are you scared?" As he spoke, he turned to look at her, his chin smoothly grazing her nipple as he lifted his head.

Looking into his eyes, she could see that an admission wasn't required as he already knew the answer. "Think of it as inspiration." He lay his head back down. "If I'm your muse, that's my job."

Yvonne almost laughed, her chest briefly thrusting upwards, the stifling of her chuckle seeming like a hiccup.

Lazily raising his head enough for his dreads to brush her skin, Garvey observed her, only one eye open. "What's wrong?"

She offered an easy smile and shook her head. "Nothing."

He returned to his relaxed state and lounging position, using her body as if she were a comfortable pillow.

Looking down at his hair, his face only partially visible, Yvonne marvelled at how he looked so unlike the whirlwind that he was. Blowing into her life without warning, he had turned it around.

Surrendering to her heavy eyelids, Yvonne began to drift as if led by Garvey's exhaustion.

Her last thought was that he had caused no disaster. Despite the complete change he had wrought in her and her life the moment he entered it, the tumultuous outcome she would have expected had failed to materialise. Rather than the chaos and destruction that should come with such a storm, Hurricane Garvey had picked everything up and dropped it back down in a position that proved to be better than before.

I hope he doesn't really expect me to wear just paint.

Chapter Five

Standing there naked would have been strange enough, but being watched intensified the feelings further. Starting at her toes, his eyes swept slowly up her body, studying every inch of her before looking into her eyes. Initially, she had to fight to resist covering herself up, but the desire dissipated as his powerful gaze warmed her body.

"Beautiful."

The softly uttered word carried through the silence of the room, reverberating through her body until her clit throbbed.

Yvonne was so used to his casual appearance that she was initially taken aback by seeing Garvey in a suit. He gave the impression that he lived in the informal clothes he had worn every time he'd been at her home. It made the new formal look an unusual sight, but the ensemble couldn't have suited him more. He still managed to successfully display his personality in what could have been a boring black suit by coupling it with a blood-red shirt. His dreads hanging down his back added a further touch of rebellion.

By comparison, Yvonne dressed more demurely in a full-skirted black dress, the rarely worn underskirt feeling strange against her legs. She had opted for a pair of gold shoes as a small nod to it being a special occasion, in addition to the sequins that decorated the shoulder straps. The fact that their effect was lost under the shrug she wore didn't enter her mind — it was the dress she wanted to wear, yet she still wanted to cover her arms.

Her outfit succeeded in earning her an appreciative smile. "You look absolutely beautiful."

The doubt that had plagued her while she'd been dressing instantly dissipated with those few words. She smiled gratefully, self-consciously sweeping her hands over her waist and down her skirt.

"Thank you. You look amazing," she gushed, before stopping to accept his greeting kiss, the gentle touch to her lips creating a thrill. "You look so smart."

His shy smile came with a slight shrug. "I can't stand up nex' to you lookin' like a roughneck."

"You certainly don't look like a roughneck — you look gorgeous."

The couple remained in the doorway for several minutes, Yvonne revelling in the delight that came from seeing Garvey's outfit. Finally, he suggested she get her coat, raising once again the nerves she had felt when she was getting ready.

After helping her on with her coat, Garvey took her hand after patiently waiting for her to button it up.

"This is how close I gon' be all night," he confirmed, playfully nudging her shoulder for good measure.

Smiling as the butterflies slowly floated away, the fluttering feeling was replaced with a satisfying feeling of trust. "Okay."

He continued to hold her hand as he led her to a waiting car, the driver silent and patient behind the idling engine.

Opening the rear door of the silver saloon car, he ushered her in before following and turning to her. "I hope you will enjoy it."

His words passed her by as he slid across the seat to be closer to her, turning his body to nestle against her side. Cocooned with him in the back of the car, it felt like the driver wasn't there as they spoke to each other in hushed tones. Their proximity needed nothing more than that, their soft voices coupled with soft touches, an unnecessary but enjoyable addition to the conversation.

Simply being in his company was enough to make her forget about their destination, dissipating the nerves she had previously felt.

Garvey stroked her hair, smoothly trailing his fingers along the tendrils that were too short to have been swept up into her up-do.

Looking into his eyes, she studied the dark pools as if they were alone and weren't cruising through the London streets. Her gaze slowly drifted downwards, allowing her to alight on what looked like a piece of fluff on his jaw. Gently brushing her thumb across his firm skin was enough to dislodge it.

"I think I know where it came from." He leant back to reach into the inside pocket of his suit jacket, withdrawing a black eye mask.

It served to return her thoughts to the pictures she had seen on the website, a room full of smiling people with their identities hidden behind masks. The stiffened felt would have looked like that used by a superhero were it not for the gold sequins bordering it and the fluffy black feathers adorning one side.

Laughing with delight, Yvonne unfurled the ribbon at either side, letting them hang loose as she held it up to her face. "How do I look?" she asked, pouting her lips.

"Perfect."

She laughed again, feeling a lightness that almost felt alien, carrying away her responsibility to only leave her feeling playful.

"I mus' have been reading your mind."

"What do you mean?" she asked, delicately laying the mask in her lap.

"You don't see how the mask match your outfit? Even the gold matching your sexy shoes."

Raising her leg, she crossed it over his to hold her foot in the air, circling her ankle to make the colour glint in the dim light of the car. "Oh, yes," she laughed. "Good choice."

Garvey used the opportunity to slide his hand up her leg, smoothly stroking her skin to reach beneath her dress. The tips of his fingers grazed her lace-covered labia before he turned in the driver's direction, withdrawing his hand as they melted into laughter.

Yvonne felt a sudden sense of adventure that made her feel freer than she had in a long time, warm relaxation flooding her body. "Where's yours?"

From the same pocket as before, he withdrew a black mask similar to her own, albeit without the same decorative touches. He held the mask up to his face, looking at her through the eye holes.

"You look like you're ready to fight crime."

"Don't worry, ma'am," he replied, dramatically lowering his voice. "I'll be protecting you all night."

They both laughed as they wound their way through the streets, neither paying much attention to the journey they were being taken on. All of Yvonne's focus was directed at Garvey, leaving her unaware of how long they had been travelling when they finally arrived in Surrey, slowing to turn onto a long driveway.

It had seemed like a dream up to that point, only an idea that might be put into practice at some point in the future. As the gravel crunched beneath the tyres, it suddenly became more real — they were actually approaching a large manor house as was described on the website.

The sight of the grand property caused a return of her earlier nerves. Though less severe, it was still sufficient to make her hand drift across to his lap. Peering out of the window, she unconsciously gripped his thigh, her fingers pressing into the unyielding muscle.

Garvey covered her hand with his, the warmth of his skin adding to the caress as he gently squeezed her fingers. "I gon' be at your side the whole time."

The warm relief manifested itself in a smile that she directed at him before turning back to the window. She had looked at every page of the website, returning to it on several different occasions to study all the information it contained, and the photos of the building failed to do it justice.

She could only imagine the many grand gatherings that had taken place there, the idea that she would be at one of them causing excitement to flutter in the pit of her stomach.

The sensation slowly drifted higher as she got out of the car, her heart beating faster as she took in the full extent of the imposing building. After the warmth of the car, the slight breeze felt more substantial, stroking the skin of her exposed lower legs, making her reach down to hold the hem of her coat.

Garvey stood slightly behind her, moving to her side as the sound of the engine cut through the silence.

"Aren't we paying the driver?"

"The car was pre-booked. I dealt with all that already."

She studied the contours of his face, finishing at his brown eyes, which showed him to be the picture of calm.

After slipping his own mask over his head, he helped her with hers, tying the ribbon in a bow at the back of her head.

"You ready?"

"Absolutely," she smiled, slipping her hand through the loop of his proffered arm.

Wearing heels, walking over gravel would have normally been a daunting prospect, but it held no problems, a strong feeling of security coming with his presence.

There was nothing to indicate anything unusual taking place at the grand house, the substantial door framing the couple.

The ornate hook-shaped gold doorknocker created a loud and resonant sound, despite Garvey having not put much force behind the act of seeking entrance. The door opened almost immediately, leaving Yvonne's mouth dry enough to prevent her from speaking when the door opened enough to reveal more.

Dressed like a dandy, the man who opened the door couldn't fail to attract attention. His white shirt erupted ruffles from beneath the jacket of a navy blue velvet suit, complemented by a length of white lace tied around the base of his top hat, cocked to one side.

He spread his arms wide as if he had known them for years, smiling broadly. "Welcome, both."

Yvonne immediately liked him, accepting his invitation as he ushered them in with a sweep of his arm.

"Follow me," he instructed after closing the door, his sing-song tone echoing through the space along with the click of her heels.

The couple smiled at each other before following him to the far corner of the foyer, which would have made an effective dance floor. It was dominated by a wide staircase that curved up the left wall, disappearing into the unknown.

Standing in front of an engraved, dark wood lectern, Yvonne left Garvey to converse with the dandy as she discreetly looked around. Though she had been unsure of exactly what to expect, she came to realise that she'd thought she might see people having sex in all corners the moment they entered. Somehow, the fact that it continued to look like a normal manor house was slightly unnerving.

The black-and-white tiled floor and the oversized double doors that faced the front door made *Alice in Wonderland* come to her mind, almost making her laugh as she imagined a white rabbit rushing across the entrance.

"Ah, yes, here we go — Mr Lewis and gorgeous guest."

The compliment made Yvonne turn her attention back to their host, offering a grateful smile as he looked up from the book propped up on an elaborate antique-looking lectern. "I see you haven't been to *Illicit Liaisons* before?"

The couple instinctively and simultaneously shook their heads.

"Then, let me show you around a little," he smiled, coming out from behind the wooden barrier, wearing a knowing beam that Yvonne couldn't read.

His gait was almost a trot, light and purposeful like a preened horse during dressage. "There are lockers and a coat rack here for your benefit—" He spoke as he moved, turning to the side to look at the couple who followed him. "—should you need them."

He led them to the area beneath the staircase, prompting Yvonne to free her hand from Garvey's arm in preparation. Approaching the long clothes rack, she detected the cloud of perfume that hung around it.

"There are bathrooms and showers upstairs and they have a plentiful supply of anything you might need— towels, lubes, condoms, anything," he confirmed, after asking whether he could take the couple's coats. "If you can't find it, then you just need to ask."

Yvonne smiled and nodded, swallowing down the nervous laughter that arose at the talk of contraception and accessories from the stranger. Glancing at Garvey as he assisted in removing her coat, she took a little comfort from the ease in his polite smile.

"You both look fantastic, thanks for making such an effort." Taking her coat, he hung it amongst the others.

The couple both recognised that the compliment had only come when Yvonne had taken off her coat to reveal her dress, an action that Garvey hadn't undertaken as he was devoid of outerwear.

"You look great too," Yvonne chimed, finally finding her voice, relieved to have a new topic.

Still, she meant it. With his hat cocked to one side, his efforts appeared unforced and suited to the personality that shone from him. A thin moustache linked to his thin beard, which linked to his thin sideburns, which all looked like they had been drawn on with a steady hand. However, Yvonne stood close enough to him to see that it was truly his facial hair, sure that it must be a painstaking pursuit to keep it as precise as it was, his dark hair standing out against his pale skin.

Reacting by lifting his hat to reveal slicked-back dark hair, he arced it out in front of him as he dipped low in a deep bow. "Why, thank you, young lady."

She couldn't help but chuckle, not the least because he was obviously younger than her.

"I'm Boy Blue," he advised, after watching her hang her coat. "I'll be around all night, in case you have any questions or need me for any other reason."

His voice tapered to a low rumble, letting his gaze drift up and down her body as he spoke.

"You're free to explore," he advised, leading them to the imposing double doors that had failed to produce a white rabbit or anything else. "But please do abide by the rules."

The list from the website was instantly recalled to Yvonne's mind, matters of common courtesy that she would have observed anyway. The faint sound of music became clearer as she followed him, and she became unconcerned by rules as her excitement grew, creating a strange feeling of pleasurable nervousness.

She tightened her fingers around Garvey's hand.

"Are there any questions you have at this stage?"

Garvey shook his head, as did Yvonne after glancing at him. "Oh, but I do have a question unrelated to rules."

Boy Blue's eyebrow twitched, a glint in his eye making him appear mischievous. "Go ahead."

"How did you get the name Boy Blue?"

Smiling broadly, his eyes became shimmering slits and he appeared to wink. "Many people began reciting the nursery rhyme because of my penchant for wearing blue, except I'm not that little and I prefer others to blow my horn rather than to do so myself."

Yvonne burst out laughing, tickled both by the explanation he offered in such a matter-of-fact manner and by the look of mischief in his eye.

"The most important thing…" He gripped the knobs of the large double doors. "…is to have lots of hot, lustful fun."

He flung the doors open, a quiet creak giving way to a room that seemed to sigh, releasing a breath that smelt of candles and an indistinct, sweet aroma. Boy Blue stood aside to allow them entry to the luxury of the clandestine interior.

Garvey responded, "Thank you, friend."

Yvonne could only continue to smile, laughter still bubbling in her throat.

Beyond the doors, the scene was that of a sumptuous but poorly researched period drama, the occupants having taken inspiration from different periods to design their outfits.

Compared to the foyer, the room was dimly lit, partially due to the dark wood that lined the walls. Yvonne's eyes quickly adjusted to find that the effect provided by the mismatching was still a good one.

Though there was no single aspect that could be described as unseemly, her heart began to pound as they advanced into the room full of strangers.

She attempted to look back and forth without appearing to be doing so, her neck remaining stiff as she attempted to take in the entire room immediately. She quickly found it to be an impossible task in such a large space.

The sound of the door closing behind them made Yvonne tighten her grip on his hand, moving closer to him as the other hand clasped her clutch bag as if attempting to crush it. The familiarity of the classical piano being piped into the room gave Yvonne something to concentrate on, wondering whether she had heard it before or whether it had been playing in the foyer.

In fact, she concentrated so hard that she didn't hear Garvey ask her if she was all right. All she could hear was the music and the sound of her own heels, clicking louder with every step.

Being led by Garvey gave her some comfort, not least because she would have had no idea where to go otherwise. Their approach to a table at the far right of the room allowed Yvonne to relax, the separation from the majority of patrons giving her a chance to look around properly.

The table was laden with champagne flutes filled with liquid of various colours, interspersed with large silver platters overflowing with piles of fruit and berries. After seeing Garvey reach for the fruit, Yvonne glanced over her shoulder to look at the crowd, compelled to take a closer look.

There were an array of masks worn by the guests, some held to the face by way of an attached rod, others much more elaborate than the one Yvonne wore. She was surprised that the masks proved to be such an effective disguise, despite still being able to see their eyes. She was sure that she wouldn't be able to recognise anyone without their mask, making her wonder why she had been so concerned. The longer she watched people around the room—talking, laughing and drinking like at any average social gathering—the more comfortable she became.

She was so fascinated that she failed to see Garvey's hand until it was passing her chin, his fingers offering a red grape to her mouth. "Thanks."

"I can see your mind working already."

Smiling ruefully, she nodded as she burst the fruit to fill her mouth with juice, embarrassed at having been ignoring him. She watched him, waiting for him to scan the crowd, looking for options—women closer to his age. Instead, he scanned the table before returning his gaze to her. "Do you want a drink?"

"No, thanks."

Though her body was on fire, it wasn't a sensation that she wanted to dampen. It was the manifestation of the excitement that began to build within her, caused by her vivid imagination.

There was nothing to suggest that the ballroom saw any illicit action, but this didn't prevent Yvonne picturing it. The room was large enough to prevent her from seeing the other end of it through the people that filled it. The lack of direct sight served to fuel her imagination, as did the view as she scanned the room in an attempt to catch a glimpse.

Had she not been looking closely, she would have missed the couple in the middle of the room, but she was glad that she hadn't. Their kiss was without shame, not caring who watched their passion. Similarly, no one around them seemed particularly concerned about them either. The sight was enough to arouse Yvonne, holding her enthralled until Garvey held another grape to her mouth.

Accepting the offering, she closed her lips around his fingers, gently sucking them as he slowly withdrew them from her mouth.

The act made him smile, briefly biting his bottom lip, his eyes sparkling in the dim light. "I see you like grapes?"

She puckered her lips after swallowing the fruit. "They're delicious."

The couple chuckled, the private joke leaving Yvonne sufficiently amused to be unconcerned by the movement of people around them, their privacy being encroached upon.

Though she saw the approach of the couple, Yvonne was still surprised by the, "Hi there," the woman uttered as she replaced a half-full glass with a full one. Her elaborate mask was covered with feathers, displaying only her blue eyes and her smiling red lips.

"Hello," she replied tentatively, her eyes darting to ensure that she couldn't be speaking to anyone around her.

Seeing Garvey smile and nod his greeting made her more confident that she had been right to reply.

"We saw you come in." She fluttered her eyelashes, heavy with mascara, as she reached out to a man standing slightly behind her. "And we thought we'd come and say hi."

Realising they were a couple, Yvonne offered the man the same polite greeting she had his friendly partner, taking in the idea that they had been watched since their entrance. It was the first time she had considered the possibility of them attracting attention, wondering whether the patrons were regulars. Looking to Garvey to see if he was similarly mystified, she found only a genuinely amiable expression beyond the mask, instantly soothing her.

Unsure of what else to say to continue the conversation, Yvonne confirmed, "Nice to meet you."

"And you." For a moment, it was like a normal conversation at an average social event, like there was nothing out of the ordinary. "I saw your husband feeding you grapes—mine never does that for me."

Yvonne only laughed, not wanting to confirm the mistake she had made. Looking up at Garvey, she half-expected him to do it on her behalf, but he only raised his eyebrows above his mask.

As Yvonne grinned at her 'husband', he stepped forwards and put his arm around her waist like he had just been introduced to the conversation. "She's never satisfied," he joked, rolling his eyes. "But I'm sure we'll be able to get some help with that."

Leaning across his wife, he plucked a small stem of grapes from the bunch on the platter. She tilted her head back as he brought the fruit to her lips, making her arch her neck to reach for it.

They beamed broadly before pecking each other on the lips, the woman directing her attention back to Yvonne after the quick kiss. "Have you been here before?"

Her smile seemed to come so easily, an act which automatically made Yvonne respond in the same way.

Yvonne and Garvey simultaneously replied in the negative, the single word all it took to make the woman's smile widen.

"Lovely—party virgins," she teased, chuckling along with her husband. "I'm sure you'll love it."

Surprised that they appeared to be perfectly normal, Yvonne realised that she actually did have expectations of the people she would meet, despite believing otherwise.

"I'm Lisa, by the way."

"I'm Yvonne." The words easily flowed from her mouth before she could stop them, only afterwards occurring to her that she could have made something up.

She expected an adverse reaction to her mistake, but there was none, only the standard response that came when one introduced themselves.

Garvey introduced himself as 'G' while Lisa's husband confirmed his name to be Danny, leading to them shaking hands. The awkwardness that came with overlapping their arms to reach all the necessary hands made them laugh, breaking the ice further.

The foursome stood chatting cordially, the two women making the largest contribution, unhindered by the situation being out-of-the-ordinary. The longer Yvonne looked at Lisa, the easier it was for her to see past the adornments, recognising that the brunette beyond the mask was rather ordinary.

Though she didn't know how long they had all been standing there, it was long enough for the number of people around them to have increased. It reduced the area they occupied, forcing them to stand closer together.

Their proximity made it more difficult for Yvonne to ignore the cleavage of her new companion, unable to stop her gaze sporadically drifting to the deep crevice. With her nipples brazenly displayed beneath the tight top of her dress, Yvonne was sure that she wasn't wearing a bra, her full breasts demanding attention. Even in the soft light of the room, she could see the sparkly particles of the lotion or powder that perfumed her skin with a sweet, heady scent that emanated from her as though it was natural.

Her overall appearance made Yvonne feel like her own was distinctly lacklustre by comparison.

Lisa waved her arm towards the other side of the room. "There are seats over there where we can relax—we were sitting there before. Would you like to join us?"

Yvonne looked to Garvey, the thrill of the unknown crackling through her like an errant firework.

He offered a slight nod, his easy smile suggesting he would be happy with any option she decided to take.

Yvonne wasn't entirely sure how true her words were, not convinced that they would have had a decent view of their entrance from so far across the room. However, she still agreed to the suggestion with a polite, "Okay," and a smile.

The newest couple to the club linked hands before following the two that had taken them under their wing, weaving their way through the crowd. Yvonne made a conscious effort not to look down, squaring her shoulders and returning the smiles of those who caught her eye.

While Yvonne had to work to exude an air of calm, she looked at Garvey to find that he managed it effortlessly. It made her smile, just being at his side making his serenity filter to her.

The distinct scent of sex was detectable as they got closer to their destination, leading Yvonne as if her sense of smell controlled her. Inhaling deeply, the sweet aroma filled her and flowed to every crevice within her, nudging every sliver of her being into a gentle arousal.

The step down she took into the sunken enclave in the corner stroked her swollen clit.

Sitting on one of the ornately carved throne-style chairs made Yvonne aware of the warm stickiness between her thighs, the soft cushion pressing the material of her underwear to her labia.

Feeling the liquid creeping down her walls, thick like honey, Yvonne sat with her legs tightly pressed together as if her aroused state would be noticeable otherwise.

Sitting next to her, Garvey slipped his arm over the armrest that enclosed her and into her lap. Yvonne laced her fingers with his, gripping his hand as she considered the change of surroundings.

Lisa began speaking the moment she sat opposite Yvonne, but she was too preoccupied to catch all of her words. It was a new location with more to take in, making her wish that Lisa would let her look around.

The incessant chatter continued, forcing her to turn her attention back to Lisa, nodding silently though only half-listening. Yvonne couldn't help her gaze following a woman as she walked past, her breasts on show beneath the expanse of black lace acting as the upper part of her dress.

It made her eager to see the face behind the mask, continuing to watch her as she walked beyond Garvey. Her purposeful stride took her directly to a man leaning on the edge of a large snooker table. It looked like they knew each other, like they were meant to be together, but Yvonne wasn't entirely sure that was actually the case.

Immediately nestling between his parted legs, the woman pressed against his body as he embraced her, submitting to a kiss without any words being spoken.

Yvonne remained spellbound by the amorous couple, failing to notice the look of amusement on Garvey's face. "It seems that things get going earlier than midnight."

"Oh yeah," Lisa giggled. "No one stands on ceremony here."

The comment made Yvonne recall that particular detail from the website, but she had lost all sense of time, having decided to forgo a watch.

It was clear that several other people had seen the overt display, none appearing to have the same reservations Yvonne had.

Though the couple didn't appear to mind their growing audience, Yvonne felt as if she was intruding on a private moment. Despite this, she still couldn't look away.

The couple let their lust take control, the man lifting her from her feet and spinning her around to lay her on the snooker table. Her dress rode up, exposing her legs and attracting the attention of more patrons.

The scene prompted Danny to stand, taking Lisa's hand as she followed his lead. "Are you coming over?"

Yvonne looked at her after glancing at Garvey, gripping his hand tighter. "I think we'll stay here—we've got a good view."

Lisa tilted her head to one side. "Okay, we'll be over there if you change your mind."

Preparing to respond, Yvonne was curbed from doing so on seeing Lisa move towards her, unsure of her intention. Not getting the chance to do anything other than sit stiffly, it was the position that Yvonne maintained when Lisa kissed her lips. Besides being surprised that the act had even been undertaken, she couldn't help but note the softness of her mouth, made more pleasurable by the gentle pressure. "See you later."

Turning her shocked gaze to follow her, Yvonne found her to be far less forward with Garvey. Leaning forward, she pressed a kiss to his cheek, forming her lips carefully to offer gentle pressure to his jaw. Thrilled by the sight, Yvonne wondered why she felt like she was cocooned in delicious warmth rather than the jealousy she expected.

After a seductive smile from Lisa and a wink from Danny, the couple walked away, followed by Yvonne's amazed stare. Yvonne looked to Garvey as the pair merged into the growing crowd of spectators, finding his face adorned with a broad grin, his shoulders shaking with the silent laughter of his amusement. "I can't help it," he admitted, lifting her hand to press his lips to the back of it. "I just feel so privileg' to witness a first kiss."

Hiding her embarrassment with a shy smile, Yvonne turned her gaze away from him, automatically returning to the woman on the snooker table, continuing to earn attention while being pleasured. She was in time to watch as she rose above the mass, standing on the table as if to display her unmasked face.

Yvonne noted how pretty the young woman was, enhanced by the undisguised pleasure on her face, whether from the attention of the one man or the entire crowd.

The man she had originally sought out positioned himself where his tilted face could taste her, aided by her lifting her dress to give him access.

"I can see you're popular." Garvey's words dragged her from the trance she didn't realise she was gripped by, making her turn to him as the man's mouth cupped the brazen woman's eager folds.

The unseen puzzled look that crossed her face made her recognise the mask that remained on her face, warmth making it feel restrictive. "What do you mean?" she asked, briefly lifting the mask away from her skin as if that would be sufficient to alleviate the pressure of her increased temperature.

Turning his head and tilting his face upwards, he aimed his chin in the direction of the departed couple.

"They both like you."

Though she could no longer see them, Yvonne aimed her gaze where he pointed. "Both?"

Turning her gaze back to the man who continued to hold her hand, she studied his face as she tried to remember that of Danny. Almost instantly, she concluded he was rather unremarkable, especially when compared to Garvey. "He barely said a word."

"That don't matter," he assured her, an amused smile playing on his lips. "You didn't see the way the man was looking at you."

Shrugging her shoulders doubtfully, she looked at him closely, expecting to find an indication that he was merely stroking her ego.

"You a writer," he declared, as if she didn't know. "I wonder how you not more observant."

His words served as a slight that left her more willing to believe what he had deduced. Self-conscious under his gaze, Yvette directed her eyes out to the room to see that it had filled, the music now barely audible over the sounds of talking, laughter and heels on tile.

The brief glance ended with a surge of confidence, allowing her mind to clear enough to offer a defence. "It was Lisa that made the advance."

"Because she approve," came his definitive reply. "As in life, women run t'ings here."

Laughter burst from Yvonne's throat before she recognised its approach. "I never realised that was the case."

"That's why you should be glad I'm here to give you inspiration."

"My perfect muse," she suggested, nothing more than a slight smile demonstrating the adoration that surged through her to make her clit throb.

The corners of his eyes wrinkled with his modest smile, displaying a twinkle that let her know all she needed to about why she felt no jealousy. He had attended with her.

Unable to prevent her mind wandering, she considered what it was he saw in her. *Why is this gorgeous young man here with me? I bet he doesn't actually realise that I'm thirty-nine.* The temptation to question his reasoning tugged at her heart, but it became easy to resist when he spoke again to offer a suggestion.

"Let's take a look upstairs."

She readily agreed, offering a quick nod and a smile before he helped her to her feet with a firm grip.

By allowing Garvey to lead her in the opposite direction from the snooker table, Yvonne had the opportunity to take a last look at the woman who stood atop it. And she took it.

Slyly glancing over her shoulder, she drank in the sight of the woman lost in ecstasy, her head flung back as her body bucked against the mouth clamped to her pussy, strong hands gripping her arse to keep her there.

With her eyes closed, her neck stretched to offer a succession of high-pitched cries to the atmosphere, there was no way she could be aware of the effect she had on those around her.

In Yvonne, the sight of the aroused stranger stirred a feeling that she had never realised it could cause. Though she was aware of porn, even having lectured many a hormone-fuelled boy after confiscating his porn magazine, she had never considered it an option in the pursuit of pleasure. She quickly reasoned that it was because this ardour was real rather than manufactured for a camera by actors. The woman offered the possibility of reaching out to touch the smooth skin of her pale thighs, daring you not to participate in her rapture. Being up close and personal rather than removed by a television screen made Yvonne's vulva clench as lust flooded her core, making her automatically move closer to Garvey.

Pressing her body to his, Yvonne couldn't help but smile, warmed by the sense of satisfaction that came from knowing she had experienced the same act. The delicious pressure that had crashed through her body because of his tongue became more than a memory, a visceral sensation burning through her as if still seeking release.

"What's wrong?" Garvey's concern made her realise that she was trembling, the movement transferring to his firmly held digits. "Why you don't take off your jacket?"

Stopping in front of a heavy black curtain that Yvonne's hadn't noticed, Garvey gave her the opportunity she needed.

"You want me to hold it for you?" he asked in response to her hesitation.

Looking up at him, she attempted to keep her gaze on him but couldn't help it drifting back to the blonde beauty writhing for all to see. "No." Wriggling out of the jacket, she neatly folded it over her bag. "I'm fine."

"And you look *damn* fine."

Bursting out laughing, his cheeky grin extended her amusement until it rose from her belly, the butterflies of earlier becoming a mere memory. "Thanks," she grinned, mirroring his wide smile.

They remained that way during an extended period, content to simply shine smiles and hungry gazes at each other. Finally, Garvey broke the comfortable interval by pulling the curtain aside, revealing a staircase not nearly as grand as that in the entrance.

Marvelling at the powerful feeling of pride that swelled in her chest from being at his side, she walked past him only to lose her footing and stumble on the first step. The strength of Garvey's arm was immediately felt at her waist, likely preventing a fall, cradling the small of her back. With a light chuckle, she confirmed that she was unhurt and was faintly embarrassed, but Garvey's support was immovable. Garvey offered a quiet, "I got you."

The couple remained as one as they traversed the dimly-lit, narrow staircase, Yvonne's heels clunking noisily against the wood underfoot.

Sumptuously decorated in red and gold, the upper floor appeared to be designed for only one purpose, demonstrated by a painting at the top of the stairs. The gold-framed image depicted a woman, at ease with her nakedness while reclining on a chaise lounge. Her pale skin stood out prominently against the deep red of the seat cushions of the chaise, which was oversized even for her voluptuous form.

Initially, Yvonne assumed that her slight smile was one of confidence, but thought differently once she got close enough to study the painting properly. It would have been easy to miss the man in the shadows, partially visible against the dark wainscoting in the background, his admiring eyes turned in the direction of the woman who gazed at the artist. Looking at the picture in its entirety turned her expression into a knowing one, making her appear to delight in his apparently secret adoration.

The painting dominated the wall upon which it hung, seeming to both act as a beacon as well as offering a warning of the salaciousness that could be expected by those who chose to proceed. It demanded attention, a wide stool below it offering an invitation to consider it further.

"You like it?" Garvey smiled, watching her as she looked at the painting.

"It's lovely," she admitted, as they continued along the passageway, before quickly adding, "but I bet you can do better."

Garvey's chuckle was cut short as they turned a corner, making Yvonne sure that he had been as surprised by the sight of the couple as she was. They were the only other people occupying the long corridor, shunning the few items of furniture for the sake of the wall. Both facing it, the slender woman was sandwiched between her man and the wall, bracing herself with her palms firmly pressed to the surface.

The skirt of her full ball gown was hitched up, held at her waist by the pressure of his body pressed to her back. Neither immediately noticed their approach, his face pressed to her neck as if he wanted to consume her, needing more even though his cock was buried deep.

Despite the location, Yvonne felt like an intruder but found it difficult to avert her gaze. Though the couple went initially unnoticed, Yvonne knew that it was only a matter of time before they were seen and it caused a nervous heat to flutter in her chest.

The furnace raged, sending heat down her arms until her fingers tingled, tightening around Garvey's hand as they headed towards the lascivious couple. Glancing at Garvey, she found an expression no longer surprised by the sight.

Holding her breath, she manoeuvred to sidle past them, pretending not to be turned on by the scent of sex that hung heavily in the air, complemented by their pleasured moans. However, the man looked up before they had the chance to pass, revealing eyes heavy with lust and a smile of pure gratification. "Good evening."

Surprised by the greeting, Yvonne froze for a fraction of a second before offering a stuttering, "Hello," contrasting with the easy smile and nod that Garvey offered.

The woman, crushed beneath the weight of her partner's body, seemed to struggle to keep her eyes open, her tight-lipped smile partially hidden by the arm of the man inside her.

Recovering her stride to continue past the amorous couple, Yvonne stepped lightly and remained silent, still feeling as though she needed to avoid disturbing them.

Fizzing with an excitement that made her giddy, Yvonne squeezed Garvey's hand as if that alone would express her feelings as well as asking him why he clearly didn't feel the same. The smile he responded with was one she had seen before—a serene grin that confirmed he took everything in his stride.

The idea that he may well have more experience suddenly occurred to her, leading her to take his reaction to their unexpected encounter with live sex as proof.

Reaching the door at the end of the passageway, Yvonne saw Garvey's expectant expression, making her wonder whether he thought her naive. She quickly convinced herself that he held her in judgement for being shocked by the scene.

Looking away from him, she turned back to the couple they had passed, satisfying her own curiosity as well as putting on a show for Garvey. Though they remained where they had been, the couple's positions had shifted to put them further on display. Whether she had pushed or he had pulled her, her arse was thrust back further than before. Her body was almost at a right angle, her palms planted firmly against the wall as his hands supported her hips.

His low growl was audible above the sharp cries that stuttered from her mouth in time with the motion of his cock as he pumped in and out of her willing crevice. The couple seemed to be presenting themselves to anyone who had the urge to watch, almost proudly inviting spectators.

Yvonne obliged with a lingering glance, which the highly-sexed man seemed to sense, turning his head to return her stare. The brief moment of eye contact made pressure strain at her nipples, spreading until her bosom felt swollen enough to burst from her dress. Exhaling deeply, she turned back to the man she desperately wanted to satisfy her smouldering desire.

After noting his single raised eyebrow, she trailed her gaze along his arm to see his fingers resting on the doorknob. The realisation that he was more concerned with the future than the past hit her like a switch had suddenly been flicked.

Holding her with his soulful dark eyes, Garvey patiently waited for her agreement, wanting confirmation of the imminent act.

Melting beneath his gaze, Yvonne felt like only her heart and clit remained solid in a body of liquid, pulsating furiously to send waves radiating outwards. Only then did the vocal pleasure of the couple begin to fade, allowing her to recognise the similar sounds from beyond the door.

Simply seeing his smile filled her with a courage she had never before felt, a mischievousness that made her feel invincible. Covering his hand with hers, Yvonne tightened her grip around his fingers to twist the doorknob and push the door. She was eager to see the sights that accompanied the sounds enticing her, sure they would offer more than the snooker table or the hallway.

The heavy door slowly swung open and Garvey stood aside, allowing her to enter ahead of him. Immediately assaulted by the unmistakable aroma of sex, she leaned against the solid wood to force it open faster, curiosity needling her and driving her forwards.

Initially, the dimly lit room offered the strange illusion of appearing empty despite the sounds coming from within. However, opening the door further revealed a large double bed in the corner behind it.

At first glance, it was difficult for Yvonne to tell exactly how many people occupied the bed. Eager hands, outstretched arms and naked bodies obscured her view, enabling her to do nothing more than recognise that there were definitely more than two.

The muscles of her pussy clenched eagerly as she led the way towards the spectacle that others enjoyed. A quick glance to her side was enough to confirm that Garvey was still there, heightening her confidence further.

Yvonne felt as though the temperature climbed as she got closer to the mass of naked and half-naked figures, all engaged in the tasks of viewing and participating.

Picking her way through the shed clothes and abandoned masks littering the floor, she took up a position where she had an improved view, diagonal to the bed. She saw that most of the attention was being lavished upon a woman in the middle of the bed, kneeling low to offer her slick cleft to the man behind her. Tightly gripping her hips, the man took full advantage of her pose by commandingly pumping his cock back and forth.

For a moment, Yvonne was almost hypnotised by the smooth motion of his shaft, her concentration causing the wet slap of flesh against flesh being the only sound she heard.

An extended piercing cry from a second woman on the bed jogged Yvonne out of her trance, allowing her to consider the rest of the scene. The vocal woman lay in front of the one having the walls of her pussy caressed by the masterful cock, her thighs spread to allow access for her own cleft to be pleasured by a female tongue. The threesome made up the links in a chain, offering a lustful thrill for each in turn.

Yvonne could barely see the woman lying on her back, blindly reaching above her head, but she could certainly hear her. Envy-inducing cries filled the room, louder than everyone else in the room put together.

Letting her gaze stray, Yvonne noticed that some of those standing around the perimeter of the bed solved their need by joining in. Eager hands pinched nipples and fingers stroked a begging clit, naked bodies and limbs writhing together in mutual pleasure.

There were so many different sights to see that it left Yvonne giddy, filled with lust that shot through her like sparks from a fire. Staring at the sight she had never before seen and never considered, she felt jealous that she had never been able to be so free, to experience pleasure so openly.

The pressure of Garvey's growing erection jolted Yvonne, surprising her back to reality when he pressed himself to her back. Reaching back, she wrapped her hand around his thigh, gripping him tightly and thrusting her bum out.

Charged by the sight before her, Yvonne was emboldened enough to turn to seek Garvey's lips. Clenching the back of his jacket in her hot grip, she tilted her pelvis to mould her body to his, pressing the growing hardness at his crotch. She caught his moan in her mouth, lost in the confines of her body to make her nipples tingle with heat.

Lips still swollen from the bruising kiss, Yvonne looked around after they released each other, quickly spying the romantic sight of a four-poster bed in the far corner.

Linking her arm through his, she led him to it, the sound of sex providing the background for their short journey. They passed another bed as they went, the occupant couple creating a scene that seemed tame compared to the previous one.

The bed they arrived at was adorned with a canopy of white muslin, too sheer to offer any real privacy, hanging down to the floor from the high beam.

"You sure?" Garvey asked as they approached. "These things see-through, you know." Raising one of the draped pieces of fabric, he exposed more of the shimmering pink bedding.

Moving around to the far side of the bed, Yvonne kicked off her shoes and pushed them into the corner, putting her bag down next to them. "I'm sure."

Climbing onto the bed dislodged her mask, obscuring her view and making her feel like it was restrictive. As Garvey joined her, she loosened the tie to pull it free, which caused a relief that made her exhale deeply.

His smile of approval was wide enough to make thin crescents of his eyes, revealed as he followed her lead. "So, you feeling free?"

The lay facing each other, their abandoned masks overlapping one another on the pillow. "How could I not with you around?"

Exhilarated by the illicit circumstances she enjoyed, she felt like it was the type of thing that only happened to other people, to characters in a story. However, the sound of his light chuckle and the touch of his lips to hers served as proof that it was her turn.

In that one moment, she could set aside many years of being staid and sensible.

Yvonne's insides melted as their kiss deepened, relishing the firm caress of his fingers on her neck and the sweet taste of his mouth.

Moving as if of its own accord, her hand reached down to stroke the hardness tenting his fly, relishing the groan he emitted.

"All for you," he breathed hoarsely, briefly taking his lips from hers.

Her arm snaked up beneath his jacket, a tight embrace allowing her to flatten her breasts to his chest.

In what seemed to become a battle of passion, Garvey came out the victor by laying her on her back with the force of his body. Yvonne conceded, looking up at the desire shining in his eyes as he took advantage of her position. With a light touch, he slipped the straps of her dress from her shoulders, kissing her naked skin.

His fingers became more insistent as he pulled the front of her dress down, pressing his lips to each exposed section of warm skin. His action continued until he exposed her breasts, the cool caress of the air followed by his warm mouth making her tremble.

The quiver intensified by travelling along her body until it reached her legs, prompting him to slide his hand up her thigh to gather her skirt, gradually exposing her tingling body to the view of strangers. The tip of his tongue circled the engorged tip of her right breast, like he needed to savour the taste of her areola before relishing the whole.

Only after treating her left side to the same treatment did Garvey raise his head, the tips of his locks teasingly tickling her shoulders.

Looking into his eyes, she wondered whether the soft expression on his face—that which made his eyelids heavy—was reflected on her own.

"You won't be able to see anything from there." He glanced over his shoulder in the direction from which they had come.

"I can see you."

The twinkle in his eyes that came with his smile filled her with a warm sense of satisfaction that made her back arch.

"You can see me whenever you want—tonight is supposed to be for your inspiration."

As he spoke, he shifted position by clambering over her, rolling her onto her side to make her face the room. "Now you can see everything."

Somehow, the sight of the other occupants of the room was made more thrilling with his erection nestled against the cleft between her cheeks, prodding her insistently.

Pushing her hips back, she pressed more firmly against his shaft until a breathy groan drifted across her ear.

He responded by drawing back, creating a gap between them to raise her skirt and see the spoils. His fingers immediately found the edge of her carefully-chosen black lace thong, tracing down into her cleft.

Her skirt remained hitched up around her waist when his strong hands held her waist, easily lifting her to put her back down onto her knees, facing the adjacent bed.

The canopy failed to obscure her view of their bed neighbours, much like it didn't for those watching her from beyond it. The feeling of Garvey's deft fingers readying her to accept his cock was different, creating a sensation that extended further than when secluded in her bedroom.

The sensational feeling made excitement course through her veins, heating her blood until it blurred her vision. Feeling the pressure of his bulbous head smoothly glide along her sodden cleft made her writhe, pushing back against him to demonstrate her yearning.

Reading her body, Garvey responded with what she wanted, wasting no time in lancing her slit until he disappeared inside her.

The cry she responded with was loud enough to draw glances, but Yvonne wouldn't have noticed. Arching her back to relish the force of the thick rod inside her, she pushed back to feel his balls crushed against her swollen labia.

The tightening of his grip at her waist had her turning her fingers into claws that sank into the bedding.

She clung to the bed as his body rocked hers, the slow motion of his hips letting him experience every inch of his shaft rubbing her walls. His slow start continued for a short period, his smooth deliberate motion allowing

Yvonne to roll her body in a wave, moving in rhythm with him.

The heat that flooded her, blasting up through her pelvis, primed her body for the pleasure that Garvey always delivered. Used to his cock, her vulva seemed ready for his flesh, her walls contracting as if trying to pull him deeper, holding on to him.

Raising her head, she looked at the bed opposite to find the number of people around it had grown.

Yvonne caught the eye of one man in particular, his dark eyes reaching her through several other pairs. Failing to hide his attention, he looked at her with unashamed lust, which left Yvonne immensely thrilled. It was a sensation like no other, filling her body with an energy that made her feel like she could do anything.

Though only her breasts were free from her dress, jumping with every plunge of his cock, Yvonne felt like she was naked, every inch of her body being studied and admired.

Being on show created a sensation like she had never felt, making her greedy for it until she wouldn't have cared if everyone in the room was watching her. Somehow, it made her dress feel tight, restricting her and preventing her from being completely open to anyone who wanted to watch.

As she experienced the sensation of the bed shaking beneath her, she imagined Garvey ripping her dress off her, his desire to expose her as strong as her own. She had to settle for a bared bosom and the glint of her wet pussy to those that moved around the bed.

The thought of giving many people pleasure with her body became a driving force, intensifying the energy that crashed through her. She lapped up the attention, craving more until she would only feel satisfied when everyone in the room was watching.

The ecstasy he offered made her lids heavy, closing her eyes against the many pairs watching her but suffering no reduction in the confidence they gave her.

Her body appreciated his caressing fingers, trails of heat remaining on her skin wherever he touched. Breathing heavily, her breath seemed to catch in her throat as his fingers spread their heat as they made their way around her body. Instantly, she knew where they were going and her clit throbbed in anticipation of his touch.

His body continued to pound hers, slamming against her cheeks with an unequivocal slap, as he drove his flesh to her centre. The instant visceral reaction was more intense than she had previously felt, the searching pads of his fingers making her body buck as they connected with the swollen bud at the peak of her folds.

In reality, the pressure he applied was slight, but Yvonne felt the sensation more keenly. Between his cock filling her deeply and the pressure of his fingers, Yvonne was on the precipice, ready to fall into the gratifying climax that only Garvey could offer.

Their audience was quickly forgotten as Yvonne dived off the edge, completely taken over by the man that she so badly desired. She arched her back as the climax slammed into her body.

The intense orgasm made her limbs quiver, her arms and legs struggling to hold her up as she suddenly became weak. The pounding rhythm, illustrated by the heavy, wet slap of his body against hers, seemed to get louder as the ecstasy grew.

Heat flooded her body like a dam had burst, rolling through every part of her until she was brimming, sending forth a cry that couldn't be ignored. The sound seemed to echo around the room, easily outdoing the growl that rumbled up from his depths.

A deluge of liquid moisture accompanied her vocal peak, building up behind the thickness of his shaft, perfectly filling her crevice like there was no other place it belonged.

Somehow, the crashing orgasm felt more intense than any before — like the first time they'd had sex, like the first time she had ever really experienced it to its fullest extent.

The motion of Garvey's body against hers only slowed as the last strains of her cry left her throat, like it released something in him that made him emit an animal growl. The sound tore through his body like a sonic blast, allowing her to hear and feel it coming before it ended in an explosion that rocked his body beyond his control.

Yvonne dragged up the covers in her grip, twisting them in tight fists as tension racked her body. It held her in her position for what seemed like an impossibly long period, her body remaining like a statue until her taut muscles gave way to uncontrollable trembling.

Her arms went first, a warm burn spreading through her shoulders and down her arms as she relaxed, the build-up of pressure previously masked by the rush of blood coursing through her. Every pulse point thumped heavily enough to make her body vibrate, the penetrating motion reaching deep and flowing through her until her knees also gave out.

At first, the sapping of her strength was of no consequence as Garvey's concrete grip held fast. However, it didn't last. Presently, Garvey slouched, falling heavily against her, and despite his outstretched arm offering some support, his weight proved too much for her to take.

Curling his body around hers as the exertion leeched his energy, their bodies remained moulded together as they collapsed onto the bed.

Breathing heavily, her sated body was alight with pleasure, flickering and jumping within her with a never-before-known excitement.

Though he only remained prone on top of her for a few seconds, it was enough to force the breath from her body. Her dress felt like swaddling cloth, tightly binding her and restricting her movement and breathing.

By clambering off her and lying on his side, Garvey made her realise that his weight was blameless, as the sensation continued when just his arm remained across her back.

Feeling the shift of her dress as his hand slowly travelled up her back, Yvonne sensed he was about to say something, though she hoped he wouldn't. Pressing her cheek to the silky cover, cool against her cheek, she thought it likely that he would check whether she was okay, his caring nature never faltering.

However, in that moment, Yvonne didn't want to speak. She wanted to do nothing more than savour the feeling of weightless that felt so natural—words were liable to spoil it. The bed became the surface of a warm sea, allowing her to float away on a current that supported every part of her pulsating body.

Facing away from him, Yvonne failed to gather the necessary energy to turn her head to show that she was okay. Instead, she lay still, the only movement an involuntary one as her thumping heart affected her entire form. Vaguely aware of her dress hitched up around her waist, the musky scent of his body tickling her nostrils, Yvonne was disinclined to cover up though the canopy offered no privacy. With her pulsating body enveloped in a haze of musk, Yvonne tried to recall the last time she had felt so depleted, so completely relaxed and satisfied that she didn't care about what was going on around her.

Fortunately, Garvey seemed to sense what she needed and left her alone, the waves strengthening as he shifted his position, remaining at her side while pretending not to be there.

Time had lost all meaning when she felt Garvey's tentative hand at the small of her back, followed by the rest of his arm as he decided that he'd given her a long enough break. Turning to find him laying on his back, facing her as if he had been waiting for her attention, Yvonne could barely believe the surge of emotion in her chest, so strong that it required a deep breath. *It can't be possible,* she thought, slowly drifting back to shore. A man she'd just met, the circumstances, the location — they weren't supposed to add up to the ache that took over her body, making her hungry for him despite him being right at her side as her clit still throbbed.

Pulling her gaze away from his, the intensity in his dark brown eyes making it difficult, she lifted her head enough to look along her body before offering him a puzzled glance.

"I covered you up," he admitted, his voice strained through his twisted neck.

Chuckling breathily as she nodded her acceptance, Yvonne pushed herself into a position to face him, the effort of shifting her body sapping the dregs of energy that remained in a hidden corner of her body. Though only a slight movement, it stirred the air enough for her to make out the scent of her own slick moisture.

Garvey moved closer before she finished the manoeuvre, cuddling up to her like it was an act he had been waiting to complete.

Nuzzling against his neck, Yvonne inhaled deeply, filling her lungs as the mere touch of his body flooded her mind with memories of hot sex. She briefly wondered how she had never before noticed that the sound of someone breathing could sound like a melody.

"There's plenty more to see." Garvey's quiet declaration came after a long period of comfortable silence, the couple's breathing occasionally interrupted by the pleasured pants and moans of the voyeurs and exhibitionists alike that occupied the room. There was a hint of suggestion in his voice despite him making no move to disengage from their embrace.

Despite his words, and knowing that others surrounded them, Yvonne was happy to stay where she was, releasing a contented sigh before she whispered, "I'm all right here."

The couple lay together for a period that neither of them could quantify, not caring about who might be watching them.

Yvonne noted the strange sexual sounds of those around her, heard above the familiar deep exhales of the man wrapped around her. Her breathing fell in line with his. She was sure that he couldn't imagine how she felt at that moment. Each tender note of pleasure caressed her, stroking her body as if the effort behind it was hers to take. It was more than Garvey's sated frame leaning against her, it was a sensation that had the gentle, intangible quality of a dream.

Despite feeling as though everyone in the room offered her a portion of their enjoyment, they were the only two people in the room, the last two people in the world. There wasn't a single thing that she would change to take away from that moment.

Her mind began to wander, considering how she would have felt if the circumstances were slightly changed. The feeling of complete freeness would surely have been improved had she been completely naked. Picturing her body on show, available to all those who wanted to admire her, made a thrill ripple across the back of her neck before escaping down her body.

Telling herself she would lie there for only a few minutes more, she was keen to see how Garvey would react when she confirmed what she wanted to do.

Succumbing to exhaustion, images played in Yvonne's mind as if on a projector screen as she closed her eyes. Some she recognised, some she didn't—those hopefully a premonition of what was to come.

Chapter Six

No matter where she looked, there was a new sight to behold –
beautiful couples dressed in finery, enclosed in sumptuous
surroundings that embodied the simmering lust that created the
atmosphere.

He took her by the arm, the heat from his body adding to her
own as he led her up the sweeping staircase. There were many
doors to choose from, a problem which she solved by opting for
the first one they encountered.

The four-poster bed that dominated the room was much larger
than an average bed, easily accommodating the five people on it
and still able to take more.

She turned to him, looking into his eyes. "Are we going to join
in?"

Cocooned in a brief period of comfortable silence,
imbued with a faint chemical odour of paint that had
become familiar, there was no reason for Yvonne to look
up from her laptop. An imperceptible force told her to
turn around, looking up to where Garvey worked behind

her. She found his soft brown eyes directed at her. "What's the matter? Are you still doubting me?"

Rotating in her chair, she abandoned the synopsis for the new story she had been writing to give him her full attention, face to face. For a moment, she was distracted by his work, smiling at the almost-finished painting that she already loved. It showed an anonymous couple, lying together in each other's arms, so tightly entwined that they were only distinguishable by the differing brown tones of their skin.

He had sought her opinion on the background, leading to a discussion on whether he should apply colour to create a setting. They concluded that the image would stand out more on the white surface, which was more desirable. She was pleased they had chosen that option as it suited the room perfectly.

Quickly dropping her smile, she pushed away any hint of glee from her face, sensing they were returning to a conversation they'd had the day before.

They had remained awake for the rest of the night after leaving the club in the early hours, discussing everything that had happened and what they had seen. Garvey had teased her about experiencing her first kiss from a woman, which Yvonne took with good grace and only slight embarrassment. Though she had been left exhausted, it had been one of the best and most memorable nights of her life. She would always remember it and she was grateful to him for giving that to her. However, Garvey had other ideas. Somehow, he was under the impression that she hadn't got enough out of the night.

After finally leaving the four-poster that had been the scene for her first ever incidence of public sex, the couple had explored the other rooms of the large house. They had watched others having sex, Garvey's fingers drifting between her thighs to stroke her engorged clit, both quickly becoming aroused enough to make them end the observation with a deep kiss, no less passionate for the patrons around them. A dimly-lit room dedicated to bondage had earned only a cursory look from the couple, the cries from those who deserved discipline making Yvonne flinch. As the night wound down, they slow-danced in the main hall, moving together as one to the sweet strains of instrumental jazz.

"I just think you could have enjoyed it more."

"Were we at the same event?" she teased, raising her eyebrows. "What else do you think should have happened?"

"You with another man."

Leaning forwards in her seat, Yvonne stared at him questioningly, the silence punctuated by a click and a whirr from her laptop.

"Yes," he asserted, seeming to read her mind. "I am being serious. I want you to myself, but I want to show you off too. I like to see your pleasure."

Her lips twitched, an almost negligible indication that they would prove ineffective in holding back the laughter that rose up from her belly.

The sound of her laughter seemed to make a grin automatically spread on Garvey's face, noticed by Yvonne though he quickly turned back to the wall. By resuming his painting of the mural, he appeared to be trying to hide his smile.

Yvonne gazed at his back, a black vest giving her a view of the muscles in his shoulders as he reached up to apply paint. She shook her head, reluctant to say anything more to continue the conversation.

"Besides," he continued, facing her just as she prepared to turn back to the laptop. "I want to inspire another story." Tilting his head, he used his chin to indicate her laptop before raising his eyebrows, his eyes taking on the mischievous glint that she had come to recognise.

Though she knew it was there, Yvonne still twisted to look where he directed, showing the screen her bemused expression. "Why would I want another man when I have you?"

His smile lifted his face, the sparkle just visible in eyes that had become half-moons. "Sometimes you have to be greedy."

Initially, she had wondered whether he was talking about her or himself, but quickly decided that he would have suggested another woman if the latter was the case. However, it did occur to her that his suggestion only came in the hope that she would return the favour.

"What else is life for if you don't get to experience new things?"

Continuing to ponder the proposal, Yvonne held him with a quiet gaze, hoping he wasn't expecting a reply to something she wasn't inclined to consider.

"Have you ever been with two men before?"

Though there was nothing in his expression to suggest the question was anything other than serious, Yvonne could only assume that he was trying to be funny and span back around to face her laptop. She positioned her fingers over the keys, knowing what she wanted to write, but did nothing more than lightly tap her right little finger without purpose.

Why is it far-fetched? Since Garvey had come into her life, there were a number of things she had experienced without ever previously considering them. This might be just another of those things that she'd thought impossible until she actually went ahead and tried it. *I had sex in front of strangers, for goodness sake!*

Having not typed a word, Yvonne tightly clasped her hands together in her lap and span back around to see Garvey leaning back to regard his work in the same effortlessly relaxed way that he did everything. His once-black jeans had become a mottled grey from untold amounts of wear and laundering, emphasised by the black of his vest. Despite looking like he had made no effort at all, he could still turn heads.

She liked watching him when he was unaware she was doing so, studying his methodical manner, so different from her original expectation that he'd be erratic. Usually, the scene was accompanied by the faint strains of a Reggae melody, background music provided by his small radio on which he kept the volume low so as not to disturb her. However, on the occasions when she was using the study while he worked, he turned it off so it wouldn't disturb their conversation.

At that moment, there was only silence, intermittently interrupted by the notes of bird song, alternating with the engine of a passing vehicle at irregular intervals.

Engrossed in his task, he appeared not even to be thinking about how to convince her that his opinion was the right one. Though he never gave the impression he would try to bend her will, she still remained silent, waiting to see whether it was just a matter of time.

The pause gave Yvonne's imagination the opportunity to run out of control, picturing what it might be like to be with two men at the same time. Not only did a sudden smile tug her lips, she felt it necessary to pull her damp hands away from each other, the heat of them becoming too much to keep them together.

Nervously rubbing her palms on her thighs, she looked down at the tight-fitting black jeans she wore, an article of clothing she had all but given up on as being inappropriate suddenly seeming perfectly suitable. Her manner of dress was just another change that had come with Garvey's arrival, like he had special powers over her and wasn't afraid to use them.

What seemed like at least ten minutes to Yvonne was actually just under two, but she was unable to remain quiet when she finally decided to agree to what he wanted. "Okay," she announced, prompting him to face her. "We can try out your idea sometime."

His smile brightened the room, making Yvonne smile with him as her heart pounded, a mixture of pleasure and trepidation over what she had agreed to.

"Good."

Feeling as if she was staring too hard, she began to turn back around, satisfied that Garvey was happy with her decision.

"Because I've invited a male friend tonight."

Yvonne froze in shock, with only a partial view of Garvey.

"Now you are joking," she insisted, sharply spinning her chair to face him properly.

Holding her panicked gaze, Garvey raised his eyebrows, a mischievous smile playing on his lips.

"Garvey! Tonight?"

Her voice turned shrill as she gripped the arms of the swivel chair, seeming to fuel Garvey's amusement to make him laugh heartily. The force of his laughter made him lean forwards, his dreads falling over his face.

"Are you lying? Is this just to see my reaction?"

Shaking his head, Garvey seemed unable to speak until his laughter began to subside. "You can cancel," he suggested, wiping his eyes. "But I don't think you want to do that."

She marvelled at his confidence, his apparent ability to know what was on her mind. If he asked her whether she was curious, she wouldn't have been able to deny it. However, in her mind, the second man was the double of Garvey, possessing all the same skills that he had to serve her body. The fact that Garvey had already chosen the man to be included in their threesome left her with a feeling of unease, her body feeling empty, as though unable to properly catch her breath.

"Who is this man?"

After dropping both his paintbrush and his smile, Garvey moved closer to her, continuing to look her in the eyes. "He's a good friend of mine and he can be trusted. He's a masseur."

"Is he only going to massage my body, then?" Yvonne asked, making an immediate attempt to picture him with only that scant information.

"He will do as much or as little as you like," he smiled, the glint in his eye returning. "He ain't pushy."

The assertion gave her a sudden attack of nerves. "What if he doesn't like me?"

Wrinkling his nose and lowering his brow, Garvey showed his derision at the question. "He'll like you."

"What if I don't like him?"

Garvey emitted a sound like the beginning of a chuckle, suggesting the question was similarly ridiculous. "You'll like him."

"How do you know?"

"You trus' me?"

Yvonne paused, though she didn't need to think about it, admiring the point he made so succinctly. "Yes, I do."

Shrugging lightly, he presented his palms as if there was nothing more to be said on the subject. "Look." He swept his arm in an arc in front of the wall. "If you're happy, I'm finished."

"It's beautiful, I really love it." Remaining silent, Garvey briefly looked at Yvonne as if reading text on her face. He then turned to look back at his work, tilting his head.

"Are you happy with it?" Yvonne asked, concerned by his reaction.

Widening his smile a little and giving a single gentle nod, Garvey offered a response entirely more humble than Yvonne expected.

"I'm gon' wash my hands," he declared, sauntering out of the room in that easy way of his.

Only when he'd left did Yvonne realise that he may have purposely tried to distract her, leaving her with questions circling in her mind. After a moment of debating whether she should keep them to herself for the time being, she remembered the most important one. "Oh, Garvey," she called out, used to his habit of leaving the bathroom door open when only washing his hands.

"Uh huh."

"What's his name?"

"Alexander."

* * * *

Expecting the chime of the doorbell didn't keep her from flinching when it came. Sitting in the living room with Garvey, Yvonne looked at him expectantly when the sound jangled her nerves. She was met with the look of a man too comfortable on the sofa to answer the door, his disinclination confirmed with a sly smile.

Realising that pushing would be fruitless, Yvonne exhaled deeply as she hurriedly got to her feet and smoothed down her carefully chosen black dress, reluctant to keep the stranger waiting. By contrast, Garvey had merely taken a shower and dressed in the same casual style that typified his image, using some of the clothes he kept at her house. A last quick glance at him was enough to let her know that he hadn't changed his mind, showing his perfect teeth with a perfectly wicked smile.

Having got used to his easy-going attitude, she'd been surprised by the sudden switch in him that arose when she began to change the bed sheets in preparation. She learnt he was more than capable of being forceful as he insisted that the spare room—not hers—be used for the night's salacious plan. She'd offered no dispute.

Flicking on the light as she walked out into the hallway, all the anxiety that had ebbed and flowed through her since Garvey's bombshell came flooding back. Stopping at the gold framed mirror hanging on the wall, Yvonne checked her reflection, glad that her carefully curled and styled hair and minimal makeup didn't require adjustment since her hands felt damp. Though she had spent the day bombarding Garvey with questions that he patiently answered, all the confidence she had gained began to dissipate. The woven strands of his reassuring words began to unravel and release the panic they had been holding back.

With each step, her heels seemed to clatter more loudly against the emerald green tiles that lined the floor, the only original feature of her Victorian house. The sharp sounds came rapidly as if she couldn't keep her feet still, mocking the thump of her heart.

Pausing at the door, she briefly wished she hadn't turned on the light as it could be seen through the glass panels of the door, reducing her preparation time by letting him know she was there.

With a last deep breath, she turned the tightly-gripped latch and slowly pulled the door inwards, leaning her head into the gap before it was open fully. Met with the sight of a tall, bald black man who looked around the same age as Garvey, Yvonne was surprised to find the concerns weighing her down were so easily alleviated.

"Good evening, Yvonne," he greeted, his London accent deep and measured and his smile warm. "I'm Alex."

Hearing her name on his lips was pleasing, if somewhat unexpected, the thought that Garvey had told him about her not having occurred to her.

Opening the door wider, the gust of cool air that rushed past her was a relief to her hot skin, the breeze seeming to recognise that she needed assistance to lower her temperature.

"Hello, Alex, nice to meet you."

Offering entry prompted Alex to raise his arm rather than step inside, and Yvonne returned his smile as she took his proffered hand, his skin soft and warm as he enclosed her fingers.

There was a hint of hesitance in his eyes that made Yvonne feel better about her own swirling emotions. She only noticed there had been any tension in his face when she saw his brows lower.

Her sudden turnaround almost made her laugh.

Their hands remained linked as Alex accepted her invitation to enter, neither of them seeming to find the gesture strange as it didn't occur to them to let go.

With a smile that matched his, Yvonne took him in, far from disappointed with the image he presented. She found herself hoping that his newly relaxed expression meant he felt the same way about her.

Darker than Garvey, Alex also had a more powerful-looking physique, seeming better suited to a career in personal training than massage. The contours of the muscles that bound his arms and shoulders were noticeable even through the clothes that he looked so smart in.

He need only scowl to be intimidating, but Yvonne still fought the need to laugh. Everything in her wanted to react like she was a little girl preparing to do something naughty — knowing that it was bad and willing to do it anyway.

Yvonne recognised and appreciated the effort he had made. His collared shirt, a two-tone shade that went from deep black to glossy grey with every movement, was open at a thick neck. His black trousers appeared to taper to shiny, square-toed shoes, wide shoulders creating an illusion as it lead to his smaller waist.

His square jaw looked as cleanly shaven as his head, leaving a fresh face with a slight sheen to his rich, dark skin.

The warmth of his hand and the spicy scent of his aftershave proved a heady combination, causing Yvonne to sway slightly. Still holding her hand, Alex cleared the doorway and pushed the door closed behind him, a simple act that confirmed that the night could commence.

Not having noticed Garvey's silent approach, the touch of his hand to her back startled her, offering support in every sense as his warm fingers brushed the bare skin of her shoulder.

"Y'all right, man?"

Yvonne relinquished Alex's hand to let him offer it to Garvey, enabling the two men to greet each other, linking their thumbs to grip hands. "I'm good, Garvey. All good."

Watching the two men, Yvonne was able to compare them, noticing that Alex was actually a little shorter than her boyfriend. Finding her mind wandering, she speculated on what hidden similarities and differences she would find between the two men, which took her into a type of trance.

What am I doing? she thought, a sudden exhale jolting her back to reality, releasing the breath that had expanded her chest. *I should be worrying about whether I can actually do this.*

"Why we stan' up in the hall?" Garvey asked laughingly, gesturing towards the living room with an outstretched arm. "Let's sit down and relax."

Both men looked at Yvonne, offering to let her lead the way. "You go ahead," Yvonne suggested, starting back down the hall towards the kitchen. "I'll just go and get us some drinks."

Grateful for the opportunity to compose herself, Yvonne hurried into the kitchen as the two men turned into the living room next door. Sliding out her best brushed steel tray from amongst the everyday ones propped against the granite counter, her trembling hand inadvertently made it clatter against the counter.

Barely able to believe she was playing a part in the situation, the sound of their deep voices drifting from the neighbouring room forced her to recognise that it was far from the dream it felt like.

The pulse in her throat throbbed out of control as she opened the fridge, enough to prevent her from going to ask Alex whether he was also a teetotaller. Instead, she decided to bring out both soft drinks and the wine she was tempted to swig straight from the bottle.

Three large wine glasses joined the bottles on the tray, leaving her with nothing more to prevent her from going to where two men waited for her. *Two men!*

Fortunately, she had become sufficiently calm that she no longer felt like she would laugh. However, she was sure that the sensation had merely travelled to her legs, making the muscles quiver. Steeling herself for the few short steps to the next room, she hoped her legs would hold out.

"Here we go," she sang, her voice sounding shrill to her own ear as she attempted to cover the clinking of the trembling glasses.

Her entry stilled their tongues, which only made her more nervous, grateful for the opportunity to set down the tray on the table for fear of dropping it. Taking the seat on the sofa next to Garvey, she glanced up at Alex on the chair opposite, her hand automatically drifting over to grip the firm thigh abutting hers.

Garvey took charge of the drinks, pouring juice for himself and wine for Yvonne and for Alex, as per his request.

The trio chatted amiably as only three friends could, though Yvonne limited her contributions to concentrate on listening. Perched on the edge of the sofa, she observed the men and listened to details about how they met, laughing along with humorous anecdotes that involved them both.

Though Alex partook of the wine, Yvonne noticed that after one sip he barely touched the glass. He looked relaxed, sitting squarely in the chair that seemed just able to accommodate his frame. Occasionally he leant forwards, as if going to pick it up, but then he would merely gesture as the conversation progressed, his hands helping to create a picture alongside the words he uttered.

His gaze flicked between the couple opposite him, seeming not to notice that the glass was even there. An intensity in his dark eyes made her timid whenever he turned his eyes in her direction, not least when his gaze lingered as if he was studying her.

If he had been nervous, there was no longer any hint of it that Yvonne could see, certainly not to the extent that he needed to drain half a glass of wine within a few minutes, as she had done.

Similarly, Garvey was his normal self — casual and calm, which was without the benefit of any alcohol at all. Inexplicably, her mind sought an answer to the question of her silent debate — whether he had ever drunk alcohol. *Who cares?* Abandoning that subject made her mind immediately turn to the issue of whether he had been involved in a threesome before. Maybe that was why he was so relaxed. She barely finished the thought before she recalled asking him that very question earlier that day.

"No, I haven't," he had assured her. "This is the first time I've had someone I wanted to inspire."

She believed him, and yet had completely forgotten he had even told her. *I must be bloody going crazy*, she mused, focussing on Alex's full glass.

Acutely aware that she was older than both of them, she was curious about why they wouldn't need the Dutch courage that she needed. Her years were supposed to make her wiser, to give her the confidence that Garvey and Alex seemed to take for granted.

The more she thought about it, the more ridiculous it seemed that she could barely enjoy an occasion that had been organised for her.

As she relaxed enough to fully benefit from the seat of the sofa, sitting back and prepared to engage more fully as if at a social gathering, Garvey laid his hand over hers to squeeze her fingers.

Turning to him, Yvonne found his gaze already directed at her, looking deep into her eyes as if he saw something in them that brought a smile to his face. Seeing him lean towards her, Yvonne automatically angled her face up to accept the kiss he expected, despite being conscious of Alex going ignored. The idea of him having nothing to do but watch made her heart flutter.

Garvey melted away any concern she had with delicate strokes of his tongue, caressing the cleft between her lips as he sought entry. More than willing to submit to the gentle pressure, Yvonne appeared to resist only for her own selfish desire.

She relished the sweet taste of his tongue as he explored her mouth, emitting a moan that was lost in the warm confines of his mouth. The sound seemed to prompt Garvey to twist his body towards her, circling her waist in a firm embrace as the kiss deepened until his lips crushed hers.

Tilting her pelvis as a warm trickle of moisture rolled down her walls, she tightened her muscles as her clit begged for attention.

As they released each other, she crossed one of her legs over the other, trying in vain to stem the tide as she attempted to put pressure on the bundle of burning nerve endings. The look of desire smouldering in Garvey's eyes made her squeeze her legs together even more tightly.

Breathing rapidly, she immediately turned her timid gaze to Alex, tugging her hem as she pretended not to be curious about his reaction. The lascivious smile that played with his lips thrilled her, causing a quiver of excitement to flow down to the very base of her spine. The hot sensation settled in her vulva, making it pulsate as her back passage contracted.

A cooling doubt flooded her body upon seeing him get to his feet, unfolding his frame to his full towering height, as she was uncertain of his next move. Her delight returned when he raised his hand, offering her his slightly cupped palm as he stepped out from behind the coffee table.

Glancing at Garvey to see a knowing smile on his face, Yvonne saw it as permission before she hesitantly reached out to accept Alex's hand. Her caution dissipated as he enveloped her hand in his gentle grasp, his skin soft and warm, standing in response to his gentle tug.

She kept her eyes on his as she stepped closer to him, almost mesmerised by their flashing, dark intensity. Anticipating the passionate gesture that he would offer — seeing it in his eyes — made her breath come more quickly through her parted lips.

Being so close to him saturated her senses — the scent and sight of his body heightening her aroused state until she was sure she could hear her own heartbeat. Moving towards her, Alex demonstrated the solidity of his muscles by pressing against her, shifting her breasts beneath her dress as his hand slipped to her waist.

Yvonne was surprised by the strength of her own yearning—she wanted to do nothing more than taste him.

Seeming to read her mind, Alex met her lips in a tender kiss that failed to correlate with his appearance. Her eyes fluttered closed as the clean scent of his body swirled through her head, seeming more potent as she probed his mouth with her eager tongue.

With a minor movement of his hips, Alex demonstrated that he had more to offer than kisses, prodding her with the hardness of his crotch. Surprise lasted momentarily, making her gasp into his mouth as her emboldened touch moved to the small of his back, slipping down to his taut left butt cheek for a quick and curious squeeze.

Yvonne was almost breathless as they released each other, a tipsy feeling making her giggle and reach up to her neck, suddenly hot enough to feel as if she was sweating.

Yvonne could see Alex's pleasure with only a single shy glimpse. It was more than his beaming smile, it shone from his face. Seeing his gaze flick to where Garvey was behind her prompted her to look over her shoulder in time to see him get to his feet. "Second door on the right."

Alex acknowledged Garvey's words with a single nod, the sweet smile that spoke volumes remaining as though the curve was the only shape his lips knew. As he passed by, he trailed his hand down her arm. His touch left a trail of tiny electric shocks from her shoulder to the tips of her fingers, which he squeezed on reaching them, lifting her arm as he moved further away.

Raising her eyebrows at Garvey, Yvonne took a deep breath as she pressed the tip of her tongue to the middle of her top lip. Feeling replete enough to burst, Yvonne knew Garvey need do nothing more than offer a smile full of cheek to make her laugh. She held in until she heard Alex's sure footsteps fading up the staircase.

"I can see from your face what the answer will be, but I wanted to make sure you still okay with everything."

Words failed Yvonne, able to do nothing but attempt to suppress her giggles by cupping her hand over her mouth.

"I told you you'd like him," Garvey added triumphantly, accepting her reaction as his answer.

Conceding with an incline of her head, Yvonne breathed through the hint of giddiness that persisted. She succeeded until she was left with only a satisfying heat spreading through her, returning her focus to Garvey.

Noting his demeanour — as calm as it always was — she wondered how he did it. Not only did he remain serene when her stomach was doing flips, he seemed to have predicted the result. *How can he know me better than I know myself?*

"Are you still okay with it?" She had been so consumed by her own feelings that the idea of him having a different opinion, different ideas, had only just occurred to her.

"Yeah," he smiled, bobbing his head in his casual way that had become so familiar, making his locks sway. "Of course."

Breathing a sigh of relief, Yvonne trusted his words, reading the truth in his eyes.

"You ready?" Stretching out his arm, Garvey offered to take her hand.

Nodding her reply, Yvonne placed her hand in his, taking comfort from his sure grip and warm skin.

Their hands remained linked as Garvey led the way out of the room. Yvonne's heart thudded with excitement as she followed closely behind him, walking up the stairs and into the unknown.

Chapter Seven

Tightly gripping his hand, she walked into the room with him, reluctant to let him go, despite feeling the moisture that came with the start of a sweaty palm.

The only woman in a room full of men, she was spoilt for choice – her eyes darting back and forth, unable to settle on any one view. She caught the eye of a man who gazed at her intensely, displaying his brazen stare by pushing back the dark hair that hung over his eye, raking his fingers back through his thick shoulder-length locks.

Seeing that she continued to watch him, he made an obvious attempt to hold her attention by lifting his shirt over his head, revealing a taut torso that glistened despite the dim light.

Not to be outdone, another man came into her view to do the same, luring her by displaying his muscle-strapped physique.

No longer concerned about her damp palms, she turned to her husband as she pictured their imminent future.

With a glint in his eye, he beamed a mischievous grin, one corner of his lips lifting higher than the other. "Which one do you want?"

She saw Alex before he saw her, watched his fleeting gaze alight on Garvey only just before seeing her. His gaze swept up and down her form, and he seemed suddenly unable to see the man whose hand she still held. However, it was impossible to judge him — she couldn't take her eyes off him as she advanced to the middle of the bedroom, feeling as if she was in a foreign place. The room no longer felt like it was in her house. It had taken on a completely different atmosphere — one she had never felt before.

Sitting on the edge of the foot of the bed, facing the newly entered couple, Alex appeared perfectly relaxed, his arms stretched out behind him to prop up his formidable body. He had taken off his shirt, leaving it neatly draped over the arm of a chair.

The soft light from a side lamp made his skin gleam, highlighting the contours of the muscle sculpting his body. It could have been a trick of the light that made him look more developed than he truly was, but she was no less taken with him.

Releasing her hand, Garvey proceeded to undress, quickly reaching the same stage as Alex by pulling off his T-shirt.

Watching him reveal his upper body, time seemed to move in slow motion as his fit, lean frame came into view. Though she was tempted to run her fingers along the ripples on his abdomen, his action made her conscious of the fact that she should follow suit and undress as well. A sudden attack of shyness made her shoes her first consideration, which then made her question why she had worn them in the first place. *Why am I thinking about something so ridiculous? There are two men here!*

Shucking off her shoes, she stepped out of them and left them where they stood, not wanting to move away from either of the two men.

"I'll be back," Garvey informed, walking out of the room without offering an explanation.

Watching him leave, Yvonne felt curious concern as butterflies fluttered in her stomach. Hearing his footsteps descending the staircase was little comfort as it answered none of her questions.

Suddenly, the sensation of them only being able to see each other was a reality, one in which he wanted to take the lead.

Yvonne hesitated and he patted the bed next to him, offering her a seat on an unfamiliar bed covering, a new faux fur throw she had spread out especially for the occasion.

No rules had been discussed, leaving Yvonne unsure as to whether she was doing something wrong by taking any action without Garvey in the room.

His gaze was like a warm current of air, caressing her skin before extending into the rest of the room, raising her temperature to a level that seemed inexplicable. Soon, her doubts were forced into submission by her body, her knees beginning to buckle and making it necessary for her sit down.

Her dress rode up as she sat where Alex had indicated, the soft texture of the fake fur forcing it up and gently brushing the back of her thighs.

Alex immediately closed the small gap that she'd left between them, turning to her as he shuffled closer, leaving her in no doubt that the light hadn't been playing tricks.

Her breath caught in her throat as the solid wall of muscle covering his chest pressed against her arm, giving her only a gentle nudge for all the strength he obviously possessed.

Yvonne sat rigidly, her breath returning in short rapid bursts, his focussed attention powerful enough to make all her faculties disappear. The side of her body where he sat burned like her profile was aimed at a blazing fire. Swallowing hard, she prepared to carry out the instruction to speak—to utter any words—that her brain was screaming at her, but Alex negated the need.

Pressing his open mouth to her neck, he flooded her skin with a different type of heat that melted her. "I loved kissing you," he whispered, his voice heavy with desire as he let his lips skim her skin.

She felt the gentle touch of his lips along her jaw as she slowly turned to face him, the bud between her thighs swelling to confirm it wanted more. Heavy lids left his eyes barely open, rich pools of brown just visible below his thick, black lashes.

Finally, he brushed his lips against hers, taunting her with a purposeful pressure before pulling away and making her follow. "You have beautiful lips."

She murmured, "Thank you," as the force of his mouth against hers became more insistent, as though she'd been thanking him for the imminent kiss she wanted as well as the compliment.

Alex made a deep growling sound as he melded his mouth to hers, like the kiss was a release, making him briefly grip the back of her neck to demonstrate his passion.

Sooner than Yvonne would have liked, Alex pulled away and she opened her eyes to see a dark mist in her peripheral vision. Casting her gaze upwards, she realised that it was he who had caused it. Though she didn't know from where he had produced the black silk scarf, she could see that he was attempting to cover her eyes.

Surrendering to her initial instinct, Yvonne jerked her head back to prevent him from obstructing her sight.

Alex leaned into her, meeting her lips with his before whispering, "Trust me."

His words, spoken with a gentle determination, easily made her submit to the blindfold.

The tip of his tongue stroked the full curve of her lower lip as he applied the soft fabric to her eyes, feeling each of his careful movements as he secured it by tying the ends off at the back of her head.

Numerous thoughts rushed through her head, increasing the disoriented sensation that came with her sight suddenly being taken away. *Is he going to leave as well? I want to see him – why didn't I look at him more? What is Garvey doing? They must have planned something ahead of time.*

Comforted by the continuing warmth of his torso, seemingly attached to her side, her racing heart didn't seem to recognise that she was able to relax.

Listening to his deep, even breaths, audible above her own heartbeat pounding in her ears, Yvonne found it difficult to keep her thoughts straight. Feeling his touch to her lips – though not sure whether it was his thumb or his finger – she gave up any idea of coming up with anything logical.

Waiting patiently for him to move from the corner of her mouth, she parted her lips the moment he traced along the crease between them. After tasting his skin with the tip of her tongue, she took his digit into her mouth to suck it, relishing the clean flavour of his skin.

His long slow release of breath made a quiver roll down her spine in waves, and she became elated that she could offer a man like him satisfaction.

As he lifted her hand from where it rested on her lap, she silently queried his intention before getting her answer when he pressed it to his crotch. With his hand remaining clasped over hers, she was forced to caress his erection, emitting an involuntary gasp as she felt the size of the rigid cock straining for freedom beneath his trousers.

The firm pressure of her palm remained after he removed his hand, his vocal reaction coming in the form of a satisfying groan that renewed her desire to admire his body with more than her hands.

Thinking she heard footsteps, Yvonne turned towards the sound, though she couldn't see whether she was right or not. With Alex remaining at her side, a light clacking sound from the middle of the room left her sure that Garvey had returned.

Alex moved away, leaving her alone, waiting and wondering.

The silence quickly grew oppressive, the occasional shuffling too insignificant to be sufficiently satisfactory. She felt the distinct sense of being watched — maybe by one pair of eyes, maybe by two — but she definitely felt it.

For a moment, sitting there doing nothing made her feel ridiculous, the pit of her stomach fluttering with the nervousness that came with being on display. Sure that Garvey had made a silent return to the room, her mind reeled with questions as she speculated about what the two men were doing, quickly concluding that they were conspiring against her.

"What's happening?" she finally asked in a strangled voice, the sound of nothing creeping into her skin and making it feel never-ending.

Almost immediately, the gentle touch from anonymous fingers warmly gripped her hand, raising her to her feet. The moment she was released, Yvonne felt the smooth touch of a hand running up her thigh, though she couldn't be sure it was the same one.

Initially, she could have sworn that she heard the breathing of both men, but it seemed to become one. It quickly became of little consequence as the hand at her thigh gradually moved upwards, gathering her dress and taking it higher.

A flicker of tension skipped across her muscles, making her flinch as eager hands lifted her dress, forcing her to raise her arms to allow herself to be undressed.

With it being a special occasion, Yvonne had chosen one of her nicer underwear sets — black lace decorated with gold-coloured thread. She had admired her reflection for longer than normal after she had put it on, happy with what she saw. However, knowing that she was being watched by a fresh pair of eyes thumped at her confidence, making room for the same insecurity she had felt when she'd first had sex with Garvey.

"Beautiful." The single, quietly-uttered word made her jump, partly because it came after several long minutes of silence and partly because it was in Alex's voice.

It was enough to enable her to identify his position next to her, which confirmed his role as the man who had taken off her dress. A smile twitched on her lips but was kissed away before it could develop by a demanding mouth and tongue that seemed desperate to taste her, prepared to bruise her lips in the process. Yvonne immediately knew it was Garvey, his kiss and touch immediately familiar. Reaching her arms up, she massaged his shoulders before gripping tightly to hold her body to his.

She had barely got a secure grip before he lifted her from her feet, sweeping her up into the air with ease, his strong hands clasping her waist. The swift ride that made her gasp was over almost before it had begun, ending when he laid her on the bed.

Sinking into the pile of the fake fur, she settled into the soft cocoon, savouring the feel of it against her back as she waited for what was to come.

She didn't need to wait long.

One swipe of a powerful hand forced her legs apart, pressing against her inner thigh to widen the gap. A pair of lips followed, starting at her inner ankle and gradually working upwards. She found it impossible to determine who the mouth belonged to, the kisses, licks and sucks possible from either of the two men she had at her disposal.

There was no time to decipher any clues before she felt the bed shift, the weight of the second man at her side. Knowing he was close — whoever he was — made her skin prickle with anticipation, had her turning in his direction though she could only see darkness.

For a moment, Yvonne felt like the experience was a vivid dream, unable to comprehend any other way that she would be able to enjoy the attention of two men.

The second pair of lips was suddenly at her cleavage, gently kissing each breast before nuzzling the cleft, an act that revealed nothing. It would have been so easy to reach out and discover who was who simply with the power of touch — the logical step to take. However, Yvonne kept her hands at her sides as if abiding by an unspoken rule, her nails unconsciously raking through the soft strands she lay on as if trying to alleviate her impatience.

The mouth at her leg climbed higher, offering the same delicious sensations as the first, a ravenous mouth that was attempting to consume her whole. Suddenly, the clue she needed skipped along her thigh as he turned to treat her twin thigh to the same stimulating conduct as the first.

Though it was only a light swipe of his hair, she still felt it and could picture the image of Garvey, his dreads neatly tied back, nestled between her thighs.

At her chest, the man whom she now knew was Alex made her breath quicken as he kissed a trail up the centre of her décolletage. Releasing a heavy sigh, Yvonne leant back to stretch her neck as he neared its delicate skin, surprised at her own eagerness.

Between the sound of their deep breaths and the occasional creak of the bed as they moved, Yvonne was on tenterhooks, the yearning for both of the men clawing demandingly at her. Much like Garvey had suggested, she was greedy for everything each had to give.

Reading her signal, Alex's mouth met the sensitised skin of her neck, each of his fluttering kisses making her heart thump harder until it developed the power to shake her entire form, making her tremble like the skin of a drum.

Rolling her head forwards as he made it to her face, she hungrily sought his mouth, knowing he was close by the caress of his breath warming her lips.

For several long seconds, Alex maintained his position just out of her reach, torturing her by withholding what she craved.

Her desperation made her lean up to meet him, her crooked fingers digging into the bedding as she blindly sought his mouth. She was rewarded with a fleeting kiss, a gentle touch of his lips that wasn't sufficient to offer her any satisfaction.

The weight of his body remained at her side, making Yvonne aware that he was still there, which prevented her from giving up. Instead, she advanced by tilting further forwards, determined to get what she wanted. She succeeded in getting more than she expected when her progress was hindered, her arm touching a solid wall of heat that she immediately recognised as his chest. The suspicion that flickered through her mind was enough to make her lift her arm, stretching far enough to feel the naked skin of his shaft weighing heavily on the back of her hand.

With her last visual image of them being whilst they were half dressed, she released a gasp at finding that he was naked. Though, if she had thought about it, she could have predicted as much, but that would only have been the case in ordinary circumstances. And the circumstances were far from ordinary.

Her surprise, however, failed to give way to hesitation as she twisted her wrist, briefly letting his shaft nestle in her palm before curling her fingers around his girth. The thrill of literally having a man she had just met in the palm of her hand flooded her body like a tidal wave. In mere moments and with the slightest movement of her hand against his shaft, the sensation intensified, crashing into her body with a power that caused a physical jolt. It was followed by the sound of his groan, a deep rumbling sound that rolled up from deep in his belly.

That was the moment Garvey chose to attempt to smother himself with her labia, forcing her thighs further apart as he buried his head between them. Flowing heat combined with the pressure of his lips against her clit sent a jolt through her body, making her tilt her pelvis to grind against his mouth. Alex caught her moan, covering her mouth with his just in time to muffle the sound with a deep, hungry kiss, his voice mingling with hers as his tongue snaked into her mouth.

Finally getting what she wanted, Yvonne relaxed back down into her supine position, forcing Alex along with her by sliding her loose fist to the base of his shaft before tightening her grip. Delighting in the grunt that ended in her mouth, she massaged his flesh, thick and solid in her hand, as if trying to milk him.

Bending her knees, Yvonne forcefully buried her heels into the mattress to lift her hips, fucking Garvey's mouth in time with the strokes to Alex's eager cock. Garvey responded by digging his fingers into the soft flesh of her arse, gripping her fiercely as if his passion made him desperate for more than he was getting.

Inhaling deeply, she filled her head with the intoxicating scent of his aftershave, noticing even in her excited state that it was different than before — like a freshly cut piece of an exotic wood.

Radiating heat, his body drew the touch of her free hand like metal-tipped fingers to a powerful magnet. As she caressed the contours of his warm skin, Yvonne was in awe of the intense energy that radiated from him. Smoothly stroking her palm down from his neck, she let it come to rest between the raised muscles of his chest, hypnotised by the thump of his rapid heartbeat.

Moving closer to getting what she wanted, Yvonne felt like she was floating, only her hold of Alex and Garvey's grip preventing her from rising off the bed.

All at once, Garvey released her, the sudden removal of his mouth creating an intense sense of loss that made her compensate by increasing the pressure of her grip to Alex's shaft, pumping her fist faster until a pained growl shook his throat.

Kissing her more deeply, he snaked his tongue into her mouth as she massaged his shaft, blissfully thick and heavy in her hand.

Alex pulled away before she wanted him to, making her reach lower to cup her hand around his balls, full and heavy, begging for the squeeze that she promptly gave. "Ah, fuck!"

Her giggle as she released him didn't get a chance to reach the atmosphere, snatched away the moment a strong hand gripped her jaw, turning her to face the right to deliver a possessive kiss. Submitting to the bruising lips and probing tongue that she knew to be Garvey's, she turned towards him. Without saying a word, she offered herself to him, letting him know that she was more than ready for him.

All she got for her efforts was disappointment as Garvey, like Alex, pulled away before she was ready, leaving her gaping mouth wanting more.

Breathing heavily, her body on fire as lust raged through her insides, reaching out to him was an afterthought that resulted in her fingers grazing his naked shaft, finding that he was also without clothes.

Puffing out her lips, her frustration found a route through her arousal, feeling as if she had been cheated out of seeing the two men naked. They left her adrift, flailing her arms as she groped about to find a body part to caress, no matter from which man standing at either side of the bed. They had the upper hand and failed to react to her obvious attempts, inclined to simply watch. The sudden thought that they may not be watching at all stilled her body, needled by the possibility of them having silently left the room.

They probably expected her to call out, to question their whereabouts. They had conspired to make her beg and leave her squirming.

In the silence, it seemed that all she could hear was her own heartbeat, the rapid thump gradually becoming louder until the deafening beat taunted her.

In her desperation, she reached up to the blindfold that remained pressed to her eyes. As keen as she was to find out what was happening, the thought of actually doing so made her nervous, parting her lips though she wasn't entirely sure that she could speak. She wondered how her throat could be so dry when she hadn't spoken a word in what seemed like an age.

"Leave it alone." Garvey's low voice was intense, heavy with desire as it pierced through the silence.

Obeying his instruction, Yvonne dropped her hand back to her side, a smile of relief briefly arising at knowing he remained to her right. However, the unexpected command also served to highlight their refusal to speak, which irked her as she was sure it was part of the torture. With their mouths no longer occupied on her body, they had no excuse, yet they remained quiet.

Turning her head in his direction, she hoped he would say something more, her hand drifting towards him across the double bed.

She found nothing but air in the continued silence, and had no chance to search further before her attentions were demanded by an object gently brushing up her left arm, an item she immediately recognised as a feather. Both the surprise and the ticklish sensation worked together to make her snatch her arm away, shying away from what would leave her body jumping.

Undeterred, the feather—which she was sure was held by Alex—continued over the curve of her shoulder until it reached her neck. She twisted against the light, feathery strokes that seemed to saw at both sides of her neck, successive high-pitched whimpers escaping her lips as she tried to escape the torturous play.

She failed in her attempt as the tip of the feather travelled downwards, stroking a trail along the centre of her body to make it undulate, as if it had the power to control her form.

He—whoever he was—gave her a reprieve by stopping at her belly button, the tight circle he drew around the sensitive port somehow soothing. The slow gentle motion continued as the fingers of the second pair of hands gripped the waistband of her knickers. A sharp tug pulled them down over the curve of her bum before she had the chance to manoeuvre her body to assist him.

As her knickers were dragged closer to her ankles, Yvonne began to fret about the possibility of the feather being stroked up her leg. She had no doubt that even the slightest touch of the fluffy strands to her labia would cause her entire body to spring into the air.

Exposed to view, the slick moisture coating her opening caught the coolness in the air, a quiver shaking her body as the feather simultaneously drifted higher. She quickly found that her worry was for nothing as the rush of cool air that kissed the swollen bud between her labia was too powerful to be made by a feather. It came a fraction of a second before the smooth touch of a length of material was drawn up her cleft, the resulting friction to her clit instantly exploding and making her cry out, "Oh, God."

An audible exhale followed her voice, like her arousal prompted the same from one of the two men. Spreading her thighs wider, Yvonne felt sure that they wouldn't be able to resist. *How long can they keep this up?* she silently screamed, her body arching as the second stroke arrived, hitting her with a greater intensity than before.

At the same time, the feather disappeared — a temporary cessation to allow nimble fingers to release the clasp between the cups of her bra, which slipped open with an encouraging swipe from the same fingers.

Knowing that the taut sensation gripping her nipples meant they were proud, full and tempting like ripe berries ready for plucking, she pictured her naked form from his point of view.

As an eager tongue lapped at her clit — she was sure it was Garvey's — and she opened her mouth to beg for the same treatment to her nipples. The words wouldn't come. Partially because she could barely produce the breathy moan that came as the tongue plunged between her swollen folds, and partially because she was concerned that their twisted plan was to withhold anything she asked for in their attempt to goad her.

Instead, she arched her back as the man between her thighs released a rumbling moan, making her clit vibrate until the reverberations soared through her body. A warm trickle ran down the crevice formed by the twin cheeks of her bum, her hips slowly twisting as a slight tickle took effect. Yvonne couldn't tell whether the moisture was all her own.

Tilting her head back to an almost impossible angle, she couldn't stop the plea that came at the end of a breathy cry. "Ah, please."

Before the final word tripped off her tongue, she was rewarded with the delicious wet heat of lips clamped around her areola, her bursting nipple sucked hard until pain jabbed at her breast. The stinging was worth it to earn the soothing oral manipulation that followed, passion fuelling his rapid movements — licking, sucking and nipping her breast with desperate hunger.

In the moment that came after he pulled away, she knew where he would go after the brief pause, predicting that he would offer her twin mound similar treatment. Yvonne was proven correct when the tip of his tongue flicked at her second engorged bud, the resulting tingling making her eager to find out whether he was as skilled with his hands.

She and Alex moaned in unison as Garvey pulled deeply on her clit, Alex seeming to sense the pleasure that coursed through her, rousing his own.

Each of her jagged breaths seemed matched by his, raising her temperature further. As much as she yearned for Garvey, every nerve ending within her ablaze, her desire for Alex grew until it was almost equally powerful.

No longer able to hold back, Yvonne's itchy fingers went from raking her fingers through the fur to the more satisfactory surface of the warm, bald dome at her breast. Not only was she now unconcerned about repeating the breaking of the perceived unspoken rule, discovering that she had been right about their identities made laughter bubble in her throat.

Running her damp palm from his head to his neck, Yvonne massaged his nape, firm with ropey sinew, as he continued to lick and suck. Though she had already broken the other rules, she continued to restrain herself from speaking, preferring to confirm her longing with the power of her fingers. Her restraint, however, couldn't keep an unintentional whimper from passing her lips as Garvey brought her to the brink of climax.

In the enforced darkness, she pictured his face, hearing only her own jagged breathing as her senses of touch and smell worked together to provide some benefit. Reaching down with her free hand, she pushed her fingers into the muscles of his shoulders as if attempting to knead dough. His muffled growl heightened her excitement until she felt like her body wasn't her own, suddenly bold enough to pull at his body, her fingers slipping against his sweat-slick skin. The craving she had for his mouth grew wildly — swiftly enough to shock her — until, all at once, there was nothing more important than tasting him.

Finally, he left her breasts for her mouth, the instant transfer not allowing air between their bodies to cool her swollen, saliva-wet nipples. Her body bucked as the river of lava that wound through her collided with the burn surging from her nipples.

Though her mouth was occupied by being filled with his tongue, Yvonne found herself automatically trying to voice her thanks to any deity that came to mind, such was the intensity of the release that came with the resultant explosion from the touch of his lips. Her body shuddered as her arm reached further down his back and firmly hooked over his shoulder like she was determined to hold on to what she owned.

With her gain, Yvonne was forced to take a loss as Garvey released her from the gratifying actions of his mouth, her sodden cleft pulsating with want.

Stroking downwards, she caressed the unyielding muscles in his shoulders and back as she kissed him, dragging her fingertips through the beads of sweat gathering on his back.

Her breasts were no match for his chest, her nipples like hot pebbles buried in his chest as he crushed her bosom beneath his weight.

As if the passion of their kiss and her hold on him wasn't enough, Alex reached beneath her arm to thrust his hand behind her back. He held her in a demanding clinch so tight that it forced the air from her lungs, leaving her struggling to catch her breath when Alex pulled away, apparently satisfied that he'd had his fill.

Despite the end of the kiss, his lips remained at hers, hovering as if he was drawn to the swollen pair and couldn't tear himself away. "Do you want me?" Alex teasingly murmured, his lips moving against hers as his warm breath flowed like a sweet breeze on a summer's day.

She took a deep breath, the only way that she was able to utter any words. "Oh, yes."

Instantly releasing her, Alex allowed Yvonne to flop back onto the bed, her muscles lacking the strength to hold her up. With both bodies snatched away from her, Yvonne immediately prickled with the angst that came with any premature end, making her dig her nails into the heels of her hands.

"Did I hear that right, Yvonne?" Garvey's rich, low voice was laced with a hint of something Yvonne was sure was laughter.

Turning in the direction she would be looking if she could see him, Yvonne faced the foot of the bed and waited, her breasts heaving with her pants as she tried to figure out what he wanted.

"Oh." Startled by the unexpected touch of gentle fingers, she manoeuvred her body by lifting her shoulders as she helped the unknown player slip the bra straps down her arms.

"I think she's getting demanding." Garvey's goading came as the redundant garment was pulled out from beneath her. He remained in the same position at the foot of the bed.

Slowly sliding her hand out from her side, Yvonne attempted to make contact with Alex, just wanting to brush her fingers against any part of his naked skin she could reach. "Uh huh, definitely getting handsy as well."

With only fresh air rushing through her fingers for her trouble, Yvonne thumped the bed in frustration, arching her body upwards as if her lust was attempting to escape.

Though it was only momentary, she heard the distinct sound of a stifled chuckle, which only made her grit her teeth as she marvelled at the treachery of the two men, both having enjoyed her body as much as they desired before leaving her on the brink.

Every fibre of her being screamed for her to say something scathing, letting them know how she felt. However, she got no further than the internal debate, concerned that any insolence would mean having to wait even longer.

Her body jumped involuntarily.

The light stroke of the feather to her highly sensitised nipple jolted her body so strongly she was sure she cleared the bed. Her reaction failed to deter her tormenter, who continued to trace a circle around the tip of her breast, occasionally flicking back and forth in a concerted effort to make her squirm.

"Mmm." The hum came from Alex at her side. "Real jumpy."

That chuckle again.

The frisson that rippled along her body as the feather trailed down the centre of her body was stronger than before, like her body had been awakened and every sensation was heightened.

The soft strands slowly made their way to her labia, making her clamp her legs together, knowing that she would probably explode from a single touch of the feather to the bud nestled between her folds, ready to burst. *Being fucked with a feather can't make me come!*

She quickly found that her resolve was for nothing – the strength of the hand prising her thighs apart was a match for her spent muscles.

The feather became like an electricity-conducting probe, sending a shocking current though her body. Her hips automatically lifted straight up, making her cry out, "Ah, fuck."

The continual swirl of the feather around her clit commanded her body and mind, dampening her sense of hearing until the exaggerated intake of breath was as if she heard it through a wall. "I didn't know she had such a filthy mouth."

She was sure it was Alex – but not entirely sure. She wasn't entirely sure about anything except the pressure slamming powerfully against her body like the lid on a pot boiling over.

"I think she needs cooling down." Finally, it stopped, leaving her panting and trembling, recovering enough to recognise both Garvey's voice and the fact that they had more in store.

"I think she needs restraining first, though," Alex added, a smile in his voice. "You never know what bad girls are likely to do."

Garvey hummed in agreement, a short, low rumble that allowed her to picture him nodding, though it seemed insignificant.

The cool air tickled her wetness, aiding her recovery as the bed shifted, followed by the firm thighs of whichever of the men straddled her, leaving a telling drop of moisture by stroking the head of his rigid shaft along her thigh.

Yvonne wriggled her hips, attempting to manoeuvre her pelvis to put it directly beneath his, making it easy for him to enter her — whoever he was. It quickly became apparent that he was in control and wouldn't give her what she wanted.

"Raise your arms above your head."

Garvey.

For a moment, she considered refusing the request of the man who had made the whole deliciously teasing session possible — just to see what he would do. Besides, he couldn't be considering tying her to the bed as it would be impossible. The headboard was a single expanse of wood, albeit padded and upholstered in taupe suede, but there was still nothing that he could tie her to.

Her musing apparently lasted too long as far as Garvey was concerned, making him prompt her to reply by shuffling up her body to position the length of his cock against her cleft, firmly and purposefully nudging her clit.

A gentle moan, high and breathy, escaped her lips as if of its own accord, soaring high to fill the room.

"Arms."

Raising her arms, stiff and heavy, she crossed her wrists above her head, her back automatically arching to raise her breasts as if being presented to the man that leaned over her.

Cool and smooth against her skin, fabric was tied around her wrists to secure them. It quickly warmed to her skin as Garvey withdrew, leaving her alone again. Though her movements were restricted, Yvonne silently scoffed at the idea of not being able to get out of the binding, which felt too delicate to be able to hold her.

Her chance to test the strength of the fastening came almost immediately when what felt like a pinch simultaneously snapped at both of her nipples.

"Oh, God!" she yelped, straining against the restraint that held her wrists firmly together, laying against the pillow as her arched back jerked her breasts upwards. "You two are merciless."

Though not sure whether she heard one chuckle or two, she didn't dwell on it as she had other concerns.

Recovering from the shock, she recognised that the cold sensation was caused by ice cubes being pressed to her previously hot nipples. She writhed in an attempt to escape the freezing blocks — two of them — but found her attempts wasted. While one circled her right areola, the second ice cube travelled down her abdomen, melting on the heat of her skin to leave a cool trail of water.

Though she was sure each of the men held an ice cube, they appeared to have the same idea as the cubes reached her belly button, circling it until ice-cold water filled the recess.

Melting quickly, the ice at her breast dribbled cool water down her breasts like it was coursing down the side of a mountain, tickling her skin. Yvonne breathed a sigh of relief as the ice was removed from her nipple, quickly acclimatising to the water that became warmed to her body temperature.

In the next moment, she flinched as a drop of cool water splashed against her lips, leading her to part her lips, capturing the refreshing liquid that seemed to stimulate her thirst.

Sure that it was Garvey who fed her, Yvonne felt her muscles become taut as Alex trailed downwards from the tiny well that he had left behind in her navel. Tightly pulling her stomach in, she gave a soft cry as the melting block moved lower, every movement releasing water that poured down her skin in ticklish streams.

She failed to recognise that the ice had been removed until the chill on her skin was replaced with the sensuous warmth of an open mouth. Refreshed by the ice water dripping down her throat and delighted by the sensation of water being licked and sucked off her skin, Yvonne was now completely at ease under the control of the two men.

The gentle binding stroked her skin as she strained against it, heaving her body skyward in the process of stretching her neck, reaching for the trivial amount of reviving liquid as it was withdrawn.

The moment the ice cube was lowered to her mouth, Yvonne sucked it hungrily, running her tongue over the fingers holding it, the skin cool and clean-tasting.

"Greedy." It was Garvey who made the comment, making a declaration rather than asking a question.

Yvonne pushed away the smile that played at her lips, knowing she couldn't argue. "And when are you going to satisfy my greed?"

A long, low whistle of disbelief came from Garvey's direction, while Alex chuckled, making a satisfied smile slowly curve her lips, proud of the minor act of defiance that they'd failed to predict.

"Ay, man." His voice faded as he moved away, making her brace herself for more acts designed to inflame her ardour. "See if you can satisfy the lady's greed."

Before he had finished the sentence, determined fingers dug into her left thigh to spread her legs before a biting cold smacked the swollen bud between her labia.

Sharply drawing in a breath, her body reared up as the shocking sensation coursed through her body, her hips leading the way. Stiffly arching her body like a tall bridge, all of her muscles became taut, keeping her there until she gradually became used to the adjusted temperature.

Apparently, it wasn't enough of a reaction to prevent the ice from being slipped down into her crevice, cooling the slick moisture that had settled there. The continuing chill came as she slowly lowered her body back down to the bed, only to spring back up with a sharp cry as the ice stroked her entrance. "Oh, my God!"

"She's getting religious." The softly uttered words, lightened by laughter, came from Alex's tongue, so close to her spread legs that she felt his breath further cool the moisture at her opening.

A tremor ran down her spine as he replaced the ice, the warmth of his mouth an instant and contrasting comfort.

Clamping her legs to his face, the fierce grip in which she held him made her feel as if someone else was forcing them closed. Frenzied thrusts as she took his mouth made her body feel unlike her own, barely able to understand where the strength and yearning came from.

Frustrated by her inability to get free from her bindings to hold his head, needing control to fuck his face, Yvonne lifted her legs. Whilst she had intended to drape them over his shoulders, using them to pull him close enough to prevent light passing between their bodies, she inadvertently released him before she intended to, her trembling legs refusing to cooperate.

The pleasing sound of his jagged breaths made her laugh, tempering any disappointment that came from her loss after having relinquished the upper hand.

She continued to laugh as a strong pair of hands clasped her calves, her laughter turning into a squeal as she was dragged a short distance to the foot of the bed. Cool air rushed over the moisture on her skin, her back sliding against the fur flattened by her weight, with a wet imprint left by the mixture of water and sweat.

The pounding of her heart took on a new intensity as the next unknown act made a rapid approach. Had she been prepared to query what they had planned, she wouldn't have had the chance to utter the words before she was snatched up from where she lay. The owner of the hands gripping her remained unknown, the deep breaths providing no clue as his fingers gripped her waist, making her continue to feel the forceful grip even when she had been released.

Though disoriented from being spun around, Yvonne instinctively stretched her bound arms in front of her, just in time to support her as her knees dropped to edge of the bed, preventing her from falling on her face.

On her hands and knees, her arms felt uncomfortable tied together but she wasn't about to let them know that. She suspected that she would soon — finally — discover the culmination of their sexual plot and experience the crashing orgasm that her body so desperately wanted.

The return of the ice, planted on the small of her back and aligned with her spine, made her realise that she had been holding her breath. A gasp burst from her lips, sounding like a sharp hiss.

Determined to remain steadfast, Yvonne was still until one of her tormentors slid the frozen block to the peak of her crevice. *Alex*, she decided, picturing the mystery fingers holding the melting cube. She found herself unable to match their patience as they waited for the water to roll down her cleft, straining her position as her arms began to tremble.

Tilting her pelvis, she displayed a greater portion of the gap throbbing between her legs, thrilled at the growl that came from behind her as she presented herself. A distinct rustle cut through her heavy breaths and the pounding in her ears as cool water trickled down her crevice to mingle with the sap gathering between her folds. As she wriggled beneath the sensation, she couldn't concentrate enough to identify it, yet it still heightened her anticipation.

The liquid had barely completed its route, warmed by her body until she could just feel the difference, before an insistent pair of hands suddenly grasped her hips. She immediately felt the pressure of a stiff shaft against her clit, prodding demandingly before dragging upwards to seek her entrance. A deep breath shuddered from her throat, caused by a heady mixture of relief and elation.

Her own voice masked the vocalisation of the man that smoothly entered her, aided by her wetness, so that she couldn't tell who it was. Not that she cared. The instant gratification made her body quiver as if it was singing, consuming her until the flames that flickered through her body disengaged her brain.

The force of his deep thrust propelled her forwards, making her back arch as she struggled to stay upright. White heat blasted through her with the intensity of a powerful explosion, jolting her body until her hands slid against the damp, flattened fur.

It was impossible to believe that the sensation of being completely filled by him could be bettered. Her theory disintegrated the moment the smooth sensation of hot skin rubbed across her shoulder, Alex's solid torso immediately recognisable. She felt his breath on her neck as he manoeuvred in front of her, his arm sliding into the gap beneath her body as he pressed their cheeks together.

Smothering her mouth, he captured her moans and heavy breaths with a kiss that seemed more meaningful than any they had experienced together before. As he pulled away, running his fingers across her brow and into her hair, she ached to see him, craving the look in his eyes while Garvey pounded deeper.

"What are you going to do for me if I release your wrists?" His voice was low and seductive, full of his hunger for her that she was barred from seeing, a gratifying consolation.

"Ah." An immediate response wasn't forthcoming though she was willing to offer it—her body wouldn't cooperate. The force with which Garvey fucked her from behind demanded everything she had, pounding her heart and crushing her lungs until she struggled to say, "Any—thing."

A sound like a hum and a growl combined rose before he offered words of approval. "That's what I like to hear."

Before he finished speaking, she felt his palm cup her left breast, briefly squeezing her flesh and pinching her nipple as if he couldn't resist the opportunity to caress. Stroking the back of his hand down her arm, his slow progress gave the impression he wanted to offer the full benefit of the electrical charge that crackled from his fingers.

Garvey seemed oblivious to the exchange as he continued with the solid rhythm of his hips as he pumped like a piston, each driving motion ending with his heavy sac thumping her labia.

Gaining leverage with a vice-like grip of her waist, Garvey's grasp enabled Yvonne to feel each of his digits pressing into her flesh. His ferocity made his intentions unequivocal, keeping him on her mind as she imagined reaching out to complete the chain.

In her mind, she could blindly reach out and instantly find Alex's shaft, passing on some of the pleasure that she was being given. She imagined wrapping her fingers around his rod of rigid flesh, pumping her fist as it gradually tightened around his flesh. In reality, as his deft fingers released the knot and the binding came loose, Yvonne knew her hand would be required to keep her body stable.

The scarf weaved around her wrists, stroking her skin and emphasising the quiver that shimmered across her shoulders and down her arms. Each of Garvey's thrusts became stronger than the last, jerking her bent body forwards as he reached the point that could drive her wild. She knew that she couldn't maintain her position if she lifted her hand, that doing anything more than spreading her arms further apart would make her collapse.

Garvey controlled her body, taking her ability to concentrate, distracted by Alex who remained at her side. Sensing his presence and feeling his movement, the intoxicating warm scent of his skin combining with Garvey's demand to leave her dizzy. Even in the state of ecstasy that Garvey forced on her, Yvonne was still conscious of Alex being there and the risk of him being ignored—not least because she had told him she was prepared to do anything. It quickly became apparent that Alex wasn't similarly concerned, snaking his hand through the gap created by her folded frame, sliding against the damp skin of her thigh. She imagined his fingers before she felt them, all thought of the ice's raw kiss sinking deeper into the realms of distant memory as her clit throbbed expectantly.

With his lips at her ear, Alex breathed heavily as his fingers found the bud ready to burst, pulsing frantically as if directly linked to her heart. "I love watching you." His whispered words came with the firm touch of two fingers to her clit, insistent enough to make her emit a high-pitched cry distinct from the breathy moans earned by Garvey.

"Oh, yeah," he growled, his voice tempering to a rumbling note as he began moving his fingers back and forth. "I'm jealous, I want to sink deep into your pussy."

A gasp sprang from Yvonne's throat as his fingers moved faster, his body pressed to her side as if leaving space between them was impossible. "Your body is fucking amazing."

Speaking through gritted teeth, he sounded like he was trying to restrain the longing he felt, but failed in his attempt. The speed of his fingers increased, slipping against the slick moisture within her cleft as his motion aligned with Garvey's. The two must have planned to work in unison to drive her into a state of losing control. Her arms trembled like her bones had been replaced with jelly.

"I wanna see you come."

Crashing into her body like a tidal wave, her climax seized her muscles the moment he ended his sentence, gripping her tightly and shaking her. Arching her back in a severe stretch, Yvonne failed to notice Garvey's gravelly moan or the removal of Alex's fingers. Simultaneous flashes of white heat seemed to shock her body, preventing her senses from working as they should. The heightened ability of her other senses while her sight was taken away instantly dissipated, returning her to a state of disorientation as a shudder rocked her body. No longer able to support her frame, as if all her muscles, flesh and bones had doubled in weight, Yvonne collapsed forwards onto a surface other than the bed. She immediately recognised the firm sinews of Alex's physique beneath her, tempting her curious touch with the feel of his hot, moist skin.

With only her hands to guide her, Yvonne smoothly stroked the pads of her fingers up his body, caressing the shapes, dips and valleys created by his developed abs. Trying to recall the partial image of his body from when she had first walked into the bedroom, Yvonne found that she could hardly remember what he looked like, let alone whether the muscles strapped around his torso were pronounced.

As she reached the unyielding humps on his chest, Garvey delivered a firm slap to her arse cheeks, still in the air as if presented to him.

The stroke of his fingers that fell between her cleft made a quiver curl up her spine as she fell forwards, too weak to resist the force of his hand. The gentle blow caused her to fall flat against Alex, sprawled on his body so that her clammy skin skidded over his front.

Rigid and slick, his cock pressed against her stomach, making her tighten her muscles, allowing enough of a gap to make his sheathed shaft jump and twitch against her skin.

A single heavy pulsation tightened her vulva as if signalling readiness, however, her doubts still remained. *I've come once*, she thought. *My body is satisfied – I can't come again.*

Her thoughts on the limitations of her own body intensified her desire to pleasure his, loath to leave him out. With a slight shift of her body, a syrupy sweet scent that she didn't recognise rose to her nostrils. Allowing her hands to continue to drift upwards, she relished his sharp hiss as she dragged her fingernails over his nipples, flicking the taut tips. Though it seemed so minor, the sound had an instant effect, swelling the yearning within her like a cloud of hot steam.

Refusing to be ignored, the sensation grew stronger until it pressed against her like a balloon filling with air. Barely released by a slow exhale through her pursed lips, the pressure had nowhere else to go and made her desperate to see him. Keeping one hand pressed to his chest, his skin as smooth as the band around her eyes, she scratched her forehead in her haste to drag it off. Leaving it looped around her neck, Yvonne blinked against the dim light as she gazed at him, finally able to see him in all his glory. "Naughty," he smiled, his eyes twinkling from where he lay, telling her what his body was prepared for.

The dark skin of his torso gleamed like the ripples on the moonlit surface of a lake, inviting her to dive in. Intending to do just that, she proceeded to shuffle down his body, her forearms rolling smoothly along the solid wings at his sides as she looked back at his face.

The soft coral red of the condom clinging to his shaft, the source of the sweet aroma, came into view, standing proud and making her run the tip of her tongue across her top lip.

Before getting the chance to make use of her freshly moistened lips, the firm touch of Garvey's strong hands to her hips caught her attention. Turning her head failed to offer a glimpse of him before he propelled her forwards, moving his hand to stroke the sticky swell between her folds.

The reaction of her body was instantaneous, the slight stimulation causing a river of heat to course through her body. As Alex reached down to encircle the base of his cock with a firm grip, she recognised what they expected, causing a flood of moisture to her throbbing swell.

Pushing herself up onto her knees, Yvonne looked down at Alex as the feather-light touch of Garvey's fingers followed a route down her spine. Despite the ticklish sensation making her body roll in a wave, she held the gaze of the man lying beneath her, lifting her body enough to let him guide his shaft to her entrance.

Even before the swollen head of his cock licked her cleft, she felt the heat radiating from his body, a gentle warning of the intensity she could expect. Spreading her thighs as she raised her body to the optimum pose, her vindication came as Alex released his shaft to grip her hips, aligning his cock with its destination.

His shaft firmly swept over her swollen, sated clit, sending a frisson through her core that passed over her nipples, licking them with flames that made them swell to the bursting point.

He pierced her tender and swollen pussy and she accepted his shaft to the hilt, plunging deep through the combined force of their desire, physical and mental. A sigh escaped her lips, long and deep enough to empty her lungs, before a breathy giggle followed. Amazed that her body had undertaken what had seemed impossible, she was filled with a feeling of lightness as he thrust his hips upwards, his pelvis lifting her skywards. Arching her back, Yvonne reached behind her to grip his thighs, her stuttering cry as intense as her nails digging into his skin, attempting to keep herself stable as she floated in the air. Far from secure, she found herself flying forwards as Alex dropped his hips, a sharp shriek barely leaving her lips as her arms flew through the air.

Alex reached out just in time to catch her hands, forcefully manoeuvring his fingers to lace them with hers, squeezing like he was attempting to stop the blood flow to her hands. Effortlessly supporting her weight, he balanced her teetering body as she rocked her hips. "Oh God!"

Unconcerned by the moistness of her palms, she gripped him back just as tightly as the sensation of being up in the air continued.

Gazing into the crescent slits of his eyes, the intense look she found was one she had thought she would only ever see from Garvey.

Garvey.

She was reminded of his presence by the touch of his hand to her back. He stroked upwards, leaving a trail of crackling electricity until his hand came to rest between her shoulder blades. The disturbance to the misting of sweat on her back felt like cool air in a room that had otherwise become stifling, his touch enough to heighten her senses until they felt overloaded. Hearing his deep breaths, she recognised that they had become part of the atmosphere, naturally melding with Alex's even breaths and her own high-pitched vocal delight.

Applying firm pressure to her back, Garvey directed her to lie against Alex's body, an act Alex acquiesced to by pulling her towards him, letting her arms fall to either side of his head.

Folding her body as both men desired, Yvonne slid against his hot, slick skin as he released her hands. Level with him, she looked into his eyes as he drew his fingers along the length of her arms, his gentle strokes continuing past her shoulders and along her sides, feeling his way to her bottom.

Holding her gaze as he tightened his grip upon her curved mounds, the warm glaze of Alex's eyes drew Yvonne's lips to his. Her tongue fought with his for dominance as she attempted to recognise the flavour beyond the hint of wine. She was getting high on his scent, his aftershave made more potent by the heat shimmering from his skin, tinged with a hint of musk from the sweat beading on his skin.

Her nipples triggered a reaction deep within her the moment they were pushed against his upper chest. Her adjusted position forced his shaft to her front wall, engaging a switch deep inside her that commenced a distinct sensation. It was as if a waterfall had been unleashed, cascading a shimmering flow that reached every part of her and pushed her closer to the edge.

A moan rose from her throat, muffled by his mouth as she began the gentle movement of her body on his. The smooth rocking motion of her body was accompanied by the moist smack of their bodies sliding against each other. Far from being a hindrance, her earlier sexual satisfaction seemed to concentrate her pleasure, leaving her awash with a burgeoning loss of control. It gradually swept through her like the slow trickle of thick molasses, running into every crevice on its journey and leaving behind a powerful, lasting heat. Yvonne could almost feel the flow of burning pleasure, steadily moving down to her pubis, the centre of her pleasure.

Feeling a rush of air against her moist cleft created by her bent position, she wondered whether Garvey enjoyed the scene, knowing her cheeks were spread to his view.

Though she could barely believe it—almost as if it wasn't real—she felt the approach of her climax. Tiny flashes of white heat gathered and grew as they prepared an assault on her body. She felt it coming.

The gentle force to her puckered sphincter, delivered by something slickly smooth and warm, came suddenly and made a mockery of what she thought she knew. Gasping as a hot bolt sheared through her like lightening, she tore herself away from Alex's lips with a sharp jerk.

Her arms tightened around his neck as he pulled her cheeks further apart, exposing her further as well as gaining leverage for his thrusts. Holding tightly to take over the motion her body achieved, Alex heightened her pleasure as he demanded more, making her chest pound as her lungs struggled to keep up with her gulping breaths. The furnace beneath Alex's skin was nothing compared to the fire that raged in the base of her pubis, offered by what she soon recognised as Garvey's thumb. With a firm yet gentle touch, he offered the perfect level of pressure to make explosive waves crash against her insides.

As he circled her rim, the pad of his coated digit worked nerve endings that had long been ignored and, at that moment, she had no idea why. More intense than anything she had ever felt before, the minor act increased the strength of her muscles, contracting around Alex's thick girth as he withdrew half his length then thrust deep. She felt every sensation keenly, like there was no barrier between their caresses and the seat of her pleasure.

Rubbing in a tighter circle allowed Garvey to dip into her back passage, his path aided by a slick moisture that took on the temperature of her body. She let out a whimpering cry as, with the strength of his thick thumb alone, he demanded that she respond. Even if she'd wanted to, Yvonne wouldn't have been able to offer any objection.

Burying her face against Alex's neck, his skin damp against hers, Yvonne released a high-pitched note that signified the approach of a conclusion. It was a sweet joy that could only arise with the arrival of a sensation that threatened to overwhelm her.

Above her own voice, she heard a rumble rolling up from deep in Alex's throat, her hips rocking ever faster with the help of his firm clench on her flesh.

Opening up to accept Garvey as he plunged deeper, slowly working in and out, the resultant energy combined with the stimulation provided by Alex's body creating a perfect fiction as his cock pumped solidly.

The motion of the tender sex that had gone before became part of the distant past, digit and cock inside her like they were rubbing together, making her furiously roll her hips until she brimmed with ecstasy.

"Oh, fuck, come with me, Yvonne. Ah, Yvo—" Alex was unable to finish speaking, his words snatched away by a bellow that rushed from his throat before his body was racked by a heavy shudder.

His words weren't necessary as she only heard the beginning of the sentence before she lost control of her body. Every muscle stiffened as a single shrill note introduced the temporary paralysis of her vocal cords. Besides the guttural roar from Alex as his flesh swelled with his explosive climax, the sound of Garvey's heavy breaths enhanced the rapturous heat caressing her body until she was completely enveloped.

The core of her body contracted like a strap around her midriff had been pulled tight. It kept her stiff, forcefully clutching his neck as only her muscles clutched his shaft, continually tightening and loosening like a heavy pulse.

All at once, she no longer occupied her own body, instead she floated somewhere outside it, her hearing failing as she watched the actions of the threesome.

In the silence of the euphoric haze, she felt the joy of the synchronised orgasm as Alex's hold on her grew tighter, his shaft remaining buried deep between her thighs. At the same time, she appreciated the contribution Garvey had made, watching him continue to offer gentle strokes to the passage that seemed to want to pull his thumb deeper.

Her return to reality came with a feeling of being immersed in too-hot water, soaking her until the scarf clung to her neck. The feeling of complete contentment lasted, echoing through her like the air trailing from a sonic boom, even after the conspiring men began to withdraw. Still breathing heavily, Yvonne pulled back enough that she was no longer impaled on his shaft, her sodden skin squelching against his, remaining in her coiled position as Garvey took his hand away.

A river of fire flowed along her thighs, her bent pose disliked by her muscles, but the tingling flow of impending pins and needles was no match for the hot pleasure still rolling through her. Stretching out her legs would have given her some relief, but she wanted to stay precisely where she was, contemplating her second orgasm, something she hadn't thought possible.

With her eyes closed, Yvonne knew that Garvey had joined them on feeling the bed shift. Releasing a deep sigh, he let her know that he was by her side, close to her ear.

Lying moulded to Alex, she opened her eyes to find Garvey looking at her, the barrier of Alex's face allowing her to see him with only one eye. With her distorted view, she thought she saw him wink and, with some effort, lifted her head to see him properly.

On his back, his head turned to her, his smile widened before his chest jumped with a brief chuckle.

Though she suspected his amusement came from her exhausted pleasure, she still wanted to ask, but found that she was able to produce nothing more than shuddering breaths.

A slow blink and a slight smile and he reached for her, sliding his arm to the small of her back. Though it could easily have been a connection, a desire to touch his girlfriend as she lay by his side, Yvonne reacted by lifting her trembling body off Alex. As blood began to flow through her straightened legs, she propelled her heavy frame towards Garvey as he turned to his side to await her. Mimicking his position, pressing her ultra-sensitive nipples to his chest, she kissed his smiling mouth.

"You good?" he asked, his voice husky and low.

As she nodded, she felt Alex's movement as he swung himself off the far side of the bed, earning Yvonne's gaze. She rolled into the space he vacated, still warm from his body, and twisted to follow him with her eyes. Turning to smile at her, he left her with a feeling of relief before he strode across the room, his dark skin gleaming with evidence of his exertion, further demonstrated by the sight of his spent cock as he turned out of the door.

Twisting her midriff, she manoeuvred her frame to lie on her front with her face turned to Garvey, relishing the softness of the bed covering against her skin. Spreading her legs and tilting her hips, Yvonne closed her eyes as she rolled her swollen labia against the bed, the downy hairs of her strip of hair mingling with the strands of fur.

Shuffling closer, Garvey laid his hand on her back as he nestled against her side, his body heat adding to hers, combining with the deep pulsation of her furiously pumping heart to make her head swim.

After flickering open, her eyes met with his, seeing the expression on his face — somewhere between adoration and longing — before closing again, overwhelmed with exhaustion.

"I think you have more than enough inspiration for a story." Through her sated haze, his voice was low and even, like a horn through the fog.

Yvonne summoned sufficient energy from somewhere to giggle and nod, opening her eyes briefly before they once again became too heavy to remain that way.

"Good, but that doesn't mean you can fall asleep."

Opening one eye, she looked at him curiously and found only a small, knowing smile. Not having heard Alex's return, she was surprised by the touch to her calves, confident fingers wrapping around her lower legs with Garvey still at her side. Starting on her left leg, he used both hands to manipulate her flesh, quickly working his way higher with a smooth grip-and-release motion. The soothing gesture made her release a deep sigh as Alex gave her a different type of pleasure.

Writhing against the fur throw as he reached the rear of her thigh, she expected the same treatment to her other leg as he removed his hands. In fact, she was sure that his pause was the result of a change of position as he stroked a hand up each of her inner thighs to caress her labia.

The moisture he swept back down on the tips of his fingers could have been sweat, or possibly the sticky secretions that had cascaded down her walls. She didn't care as it aided each smooth rubbing motion like massage oil.

With perfect symmetry, he stroked up over the curve of her arse cheeks, applying a firmer pressure to compress her flesh and reach deep into her muscles.

As she became used to the strange sensation, she almost laughed at the idea of having her bottom manipulated in such a manner, wondering whether it was a service he offered his massage clients. A steady stream of warm air felt along the crevice between her cheeks made her eyes open, drawing in a breath as the flow continued downwards.

"I hope you have a good memory."

Focussing her sight, she angled her gaze to find Garvey's warm eyes set on her, somehow energising her enough to make her curious.

The warm flow intensified as it reached her pussy, feeling like liquid as her legs were pushed further apart. The touch of Alex's tongue to her engorged clit made her body jolt, an audible gasp leapt from her lips before Garvey could catch it. Pushing his body downwards, he coiled into a position to cover her mouth in a smothering kiss.

Alex hummed as he plunged his tongue deep enough to taste her, mimicked by Garvey's probing tongue into her mouth.

The latter man pulled away, leaving her breathing heavily and reaching towards her neck. The scarf that had previously seemed so tight that it seemed to coil around her neck came away easily in Garvey's hand, smoothly slipping over her skin.

Lowering his lips to her ear, Garvey whispered, "There's plenty more to come, you know."

As Alex buried his face deep between the V of her legs, Yvonne knew to believe him as an intense flash of heat made her thrust her hips into the bed, creaking beneath her. She found herself hoping they would use the scarf again.

Chapter Eight

Blindly reaching out, she stretched her eager fingers to find something – anything – to caress, to grip, to squeeze. Though her blindfold prevented her from seeing exactly what was around her, she knew there were bodies to be touched. She found it impossible to tell how many pairs of hands were stroking and fondling her naked body. With fingers pinching her nipples, one in her mouth for her to suck and another crooked deep between her folds en route to the centre of her pleasure, she desperately sought to offer someone a fraction of the pleasure she was being given.

She had expected to be one of the first people there, having carefully planned the journey to arrive a little before eight o'clock. However, she found that the start time had to be wrong as the gallery was already heaving with people.

Surrounded by strangers, Yvonne tightly clutched the strap of the handbag on her shoulder, glancing around in the hope of seeing Garvey. Seeing only strangers in the gallery-like room, she tentatively advanced from the entrance vestibule, leaving the safety of the small space. Making a beeline for a familiar painting, she attempted to remain invisible as she listened to her heels on the polished parquet floor over the soft utterances of those around her.

Fortunately, it was unlike she had imagined — being the oldest person in the room amongst modern artists that she'd never heard of. The eclectic mix of people gave her some comfort, now knowing that she wouldn't stand out.

She was used to going to museums, looking at well-known pieces, but art galleries were different and she'd had no idea what to expect.

What she found was a relatively small space that was far less intimidating than she'd expected. The varnished blond wood floorboards were decorated with pock marks and streaks that seemed to form part of the design. With every pace, the echoing clack of her heels became more prominent, making her sure that she was adding to the stains.

As she weaved her way past other patrons, surreptitiously looking for the familiar face of her man, nerves began to flutter in her stomach. They didn't get the chance to take hold before the night of passion with both Garvey and Alex came to mind. It had left her exhausted, satisfied, elated, excited — so many feelings had rushed through her that it was impossible not to glean confidence from them.

They had all admitted the immense enjoyment they'd gained from the night, promising to do it again.

The preparation for Garvey's exhibition meant she hadn't seen him for several days, which left her excited about seeing him again — tinged with nervousness. The custom image he'd painted on her wall had proven to be both a comfort and a distraction, the sight of it making her think of him and preventing her from continuing with the stories he had inspired.

The work she had commissioned him for had long since been completed, which left her with a bittersweet feeling. While she loved the result, she didn't feel the same about him not being around every day. The relief that should have come from having the time to complete some work didn't materialise.

Though she hadn't known him long, her life and her home felt empty with him no longer present. They kept in touch with phone calls and emails, but it wasn't the same. They had spent so much time talking while he completed the commission. She had cooked and they had eaten together. She missed their time together. Garvey had left her with a considerable number of vivid memories that stirred her body — often at the most inappropriate times — but it wasn't the same.

Recognising that Garvey had spoilt her, she smiled ruefully to herself as she realised she would be lost if her relationship with him didn't last.

Passing an ornately engraved post that acted as a table, a thin, postcard-sized booklet caught her eye, a black and white profile photo of Garvey adorning the front. It lay there with only an empty champagne flute for company, leaving Yvonne unsure of whether she was within her rights to take it. However, it proved to be a minor concern as she furtively slid it from the table after a quick scan about her, barely breaking her stride.

For a few moments, she admired the painting — the full-sized version of an image she recalled from his website. Standing alone at the black-framed image, she glanced over her shoulder to see people milling around, considering and discussing the artwork. It left her free to peruse the acquired book, smiling on realising what it was she held.

It was a type of programme, containing information about the man who had recently come into her life, one whom she considered her boyfriend though she still knew so little about him.

Originally from Jamaica, Garvey Lewis has travelled extensively, gaining inspiration for his work along the way. It has allowed him to make a name for himself, taking the art world by storm at the age of only twenty-two.

"Twenty-two?" she whispered incredulously, a thrill pulling her lips into a smile as she turned the page.

It was a difference of eighteen years, something she never would have imagined just a few weeks previously, but now she wouldn't have it any other way.

The next page displayed an image of another of his paintings, rather than the further information about him that she was hoping for. Instead, she got to admire the piece of artwork that she had never seen before.

As she started to turn to the next page, she was startled out of doing so by the light touch of a hand at her waist. The surprise disappeared as quickly as it arose as she instinctively knew it was Garvey.

When he'd called to make sure she would be attending the event, a part of her had assumed that he was simply trying to get as many people through the door as possible. The touch of his hand was enough to alleviate the worry.

Just the sight of him was enough make her stomach flip, bringing back memories of his taut frame weighing against her, rocking against her body that he had made soft and wet.

He had abandoned his normal, casual style of attire for black trousers and a white shirt, walking the line between smart and informal with ease. Her eyes lingered on a single dreadlock loosely curled to sit on his shoulder, awaiting an opportunity to slide into the neck of his open collar.

His grip on her waist tightened as she turned to him, angling her face upwards to accept his greeting kiss. "You been here long?"

"No, I actually think I got the time wrong."

"No, no," he corrected. "I knew I would need to mix with people and I didn't want to make you stan' up by yourself. That's why I tell you eight o'clock."

She smiled warmly, instantly surprised and impressed by his forethought. It was impossible not to think about other men she had known, who were twice his age and not half as considerate. "That's kind of you."

He gave his head a slight shake, his dreads swaying as he gave the impression that he hadn't done anything out of the ordinary.

"You want a drink?" he asked, nodding his head in the direction of an approaching waiter.

On seeing Yvonne turn towards him, the waiter made a beeline for her, smiling as he presented a tray laden with slim glasses of champagne and orange juice.

She opted for the latter before Garvey declined anything. "Thank you, friend."

The waiter left the couple alone.

"I read something very interesting recently," Yvonne began after a sip of her drink.

Garvey raised his eyebrows.

"A document that reliably informs me that you're twenty-two."

Tilting his head back to release a hearty laugh, Yvonne found herself smiling along with him, though curiosity prickled her palms as she wondered what further reaction he would offer.

After his mirth faded, Garvey looked at her for a moment, his eyes intense despite the amused smile on his lips. It was sufficient to make her feel self-conscious, briefly averting her eyes as she nervously took a sip of her drink.

"What's wrong with that?"

The question forced her to consider why she had brought it up, but she wasn't entirely sure of her reasons and came to no conclusion. She could only look at him blankly.

"Why you so worried by age?"

"I'm not really," she admitted, after a moment of thought.

She recalled the feeling of the thick tip of his cock spreading her, slowly followed by the full length of his shaft. The thought made her wet, a warm sensation rolling through her pelvis as she stood there. There wasn't a chance that she would have rebuffed him if she had known his age beforehand.

"Of course not, it means nothing."

She nodded her agreement, the couple giving each other a knowing look before a guest offering compliments and congratulations to the artist interrupted them. Averting her gaze, Yvonne politely pretended not to be listening.

It reminded her of her feelings when she had first heard that he would be holding an exhibition. Though she felt she didn't know him well enough to have a right, a feeling of pride had swelled in her chest.

She was excited for him, contrasting with his own composed demeanour. It was an emotion that had persisted even as she made her way to the gallery, but she had been so taken with him that it had completely left her mind.

Garvey gratefully accepted the praise in his normal understated manner, offering quiet words of thanks.

"Are you going to show me the rest of your work?" she asked after his admirer walked away.

She was curious to see whether the process of guiding her through his work would animate him, wondering whether explaining his motivation and inspiration would display a different side to him.

"You seen this one already," he stated, nodding at the painting in front of them.

"Yes," she replied, holding out her drink to him. "It's one of the reasons I chose you."

With her hands free, Yvonne used the opportunity to slip the programme into her handbag.

"Why you keeping that?" he asked, following her actions. "You can ask me if you want to know something. I'm always gon' be here."

Zipping up her bag, she looked at his face as she accepted her drink back, seeing no indication that he recognised the significance of his words.

"I know, but I still want it. A memento from your special night."

Garvey pursed his lips and nodded. "Lemme show you the nex' one."

Pressing himself to her side and wrapping his arm around her waist, he walked her the short distance to the next framed image.

She listened intently and intermittently glanced at his face as he described his work, both leisurely and efficient as he showed her each image in turn.

The exhibition mostly consisted of paintings, but also held some photographs. They displayed images of people and places, as well as bodies as landscapes — the curved bum and lower back of a female form masquerading as a hill and valley of an anonymous countryside.

Yvonne told him how beautiful she thought the image, how clever he was to have come up with the idea, but he merely tilted his head and smiled in his normal serene way. Along the way, they were occasionally interrupted by other guests wanting to exchange a few words with the artist himself. Ever polite, Garvey would always give them his attention.

The confidence that Yvonne had gained simply from being with him meant that she didn't mind, drifting away as if remaining at his side would be an intrusion. Instead, she took the opportunity to continue on her own, strolling from one image to another to admire his work.

In addition to using various mediums, she found he used a range of different techniques to convey the message of the piece. Sometimes he played with colour, creating tones that weren't meant to be, while light was the focus in other cases, shadows and shade playing as big a part as the subject matter. In those images that contained people, some displayed the entire figure while others concentrated on only parts of it. She noticed that he was adept at taking close-up photographs of sections of the body, making it difficult to recognise and appearing to be something else. She made a mental note to tell him how impressive it all was.

"Here she is, this is Yvonne." In mid-stride on her way to the next piece, her body swayed in a slightly ungainly manner as she abandoned her plan in order to turn to Garvey's voice. "My better half and my muse."

She automatically reached out to shake the hand of the man he introduced her to, smiling politely though she barely noticed him. With Garvey standing right next to him, her eyes continually flicked to his face looking for a sign that the comment was a facetious one.

There was none, causing heat to flow down her body like a river threading through her ribs.

"This is Jonathan," he confirmed. "He owns the gallery."

Yvonne opened her mouth to say, *Nice to meet you*, but didn't get the chance before he offered a gushing greeting. "Hi, Yvonne, I'm so pleased to meet you."

Jonathan clasped both her hands in one of his, leaving her unsure of which one of them was responsible for the heat that began to flow up her arm. "I was delighted to get Garvey's last minute piece."

He released her to lay his hand on Garvey's arm, as if she didn't know who he was. "I just had to meet the woman who inspired it."

Still lost in the *better half* haze, it took Yvonne a moment to even realise that she had no idea what he was talking about. No longer floating, she looked from Jonathan to Garvey, getting satisfied smiles instead of the explanation she expected.

Peering over the thick black rims of his spectacles, he glanced at Garvey before looking back at her. "You haven't seen it yet? Oh, my gosh."

He clapped and kept his hands clasped, unadulterated glee lighting his face as Garvey laughed throatily.

Shermaine Williams

His amusement made his eyes sparkle, his smile remaining even after his chuckle trickled away. Being the only one not in on the joke was uncomfortable, but it was almost impossible to make her face display this as she felt no ill-will from either man.

"You can't keep her in suspense any longer."

Garvey reached out for her hand. "I gon' do that now."

Without knowing why, she took his hand and followed as he led her deeper into the room. *At least I'll find out what the hell they're talking about.*

Firmly gripping her hand, Garvey raised it to his chest and pulled her with him, barely giving her the chance to take her leave from Jonathan. Somehow, she felt like she had a connection to the man because he knew something that she didn't.

Allowing Garvey to pull her along, she turned around to return Jonathan's smile, adding a quick wave as she moved deeper into the room.

"Garvey, what were you two talking about?" she whispered, dodging those milling around the gallery to keep up with his long strides.

"I have to show you the best piece yet."

It was the most excited she had seen him in all the time she had known him. She walked beside him, feeling the heat from his hand as he continued to clasp it to his chest. In her haste to get her to the intended destination, they passed many pieces that she had yet to see, something that didn't appear to bother him.

"Here." He came to a stop at an alcove in the back corner of the room. "I wanted to show you my favourite piece."

Turning to him when he released her hand, Yvonne saw that the glint in his eye was still there, the tip of his tongue briefly visible as it touched his top lip before disappearing again. His lips didn't seem to know how much pleasure to show, continually moving as if unable to decide on how wide a smile to display.

He bounced on the balls of his feet, as if getting ready to run. "I only finished it last minute. Jonathan saw it before den and loved it, wanted it in with the exhibition."

Yvonne gazed at the dark wood sculpture that sat atop an opaque glass stand. It had been formed into the torso of a woman, from her shoulders to her hips. The shape of her teardrop breasts could still be seen, despite the strip of bronze that fell across the nipples. Somehow, the barrier made the woman more alluring, creating a yearning to see the unknown despite her having no desire for women. The strip of bronze coiled around her body, spiralling down like a scarf had slipped from her neck.

One end of the strip hung on her shoulder while the other ended at her hip, hanging in mid air after circling her waist, emphasising the curves. The smooth wood almost begged to be touched, but Yvonne successfully resisted as she leant forwards to look at the name card attached to the wall. *Desire Bound.*

"I was 'fraid you would cuss me so I had it put in the back."

Her enquiring glance made her eyebrows dip. "Why would I cuss you? It's very beautiful and I get the title. She is on the way to desire and she is bound up — very clever."

A puzzled look crossed his face before he broke out into a grin, his dreads swaying as he shook his head. "She? You don't see?"

Looking from his back to the statue, she recalled Jonathan's words, which made her think aloud, "I inspired it... It's...me?"

Unable to hide her surprise, the pitch of her voice rose on the final word, staring at the figure that she failed to recognise herself in. "I don't look like that," came her assertion after an extended silence.

"I wonder how you so good at writing characters when you can't recognise your own body."

Eyes staring and lips parted, she was faced with his serene expression, exuding the same matter-of-fact air that his words had been delivered with. "Really?" she laughed, covering her mouth with the disbelief that still gripped her. "I can't believe it."

"You give me the motivation to—what's the word— diversify. First time I do any sculpture."

"You've never done any before?"

"Never," he confirmed, tugging at his cuff as he held her gaze.

She looked back at the dark wood, recalling when she had stood naked in front of him, letting his paintbrush stroke her skin. It was almost impossible to believe it was actually her, that he had thought her figure worthy of immortalisation or that she looked like the statue.

"So painting me had a specific purpose?"

"Exactly. At first, it was just an excuse to get you naked, but I decided to use the beauty of your body to create my favourite piece."

Warmed by his gaze, she looked at the model of her body for longer than necessary, enjoying the feeling that came from his admiration. Looking back at him only heightened the sensation, causing her to feel slightly lightheaded before she took a breath. "So why didn't you just tie me up instead of painting on me?"

Garvey laughed, making balls of his high cheeks as he threw his head back. "So, that's the way you swing?"

She laughed with him, neither caring that their mutual amusement was loud enough to attract several glances. Nothing else mattered at that moment, except Garvey and the surprise he had revealed.

"Seriously, though. I know I coulda tie some ribbon around your body, but that wouldn't take long."

"It wouldn't take long? So, you wanted to keep me naked?" she asked, lowering her voice.

Garvey only smiled before excusing himself when his name was called. Her gaze followed him, briefly studying him from behind as he conversed with someone she didn't know.

Turning back to the likeness, the smile that instantly sprang to her face quickly turned to one of nervousness after she recalled Jonathan's words. The thought of him knowing it was her made her wonder who else did. Her fingers tightened around the strap of her handbag before she attempted a furtive look over her shoulder, imagining being watched by many pairs of eyes.

The quick glance didn't reveal any watchers, but she put that down to not looking hard enough.

"Don't worry." Not noticing his approach, Garvey's voice made her jump. "Only Jonathan knows."

"Why do you say that?" she asked, making a conscious effort to relax the muscles of her face.

"I can read you, Yvonne." His tone suggested that it was obvious, something she should have known. "It's not for sale either. I'm displaying it, but I'm keeping it for myself."

The contentment that filled her swelled her chest, made her pause, enjoying the sensation for a few moments.

"I really can't believe it—you didn't even take any photos."

"I don't need photos. You're my muse, I have everything I need up here." He tapped his finger to his temple, as if telling her what she already knew and inadvertently making her feel silly.

"You ready to go?"

Taken aback, her head flicked upwards as she stared at him. "Now?"

He tilted his head to one side. "Yeah."

"You can't leave," she replied, with an insistence that made her draw out the words. "This is your night, your exhibition."

Garvey narrowed his eyes, watching her closely before offering a pronounced shrug. "Nothin' more to do here, I did everything needed." He tugged his collar, straightening what hadn't been displaced. "You see the sculpture and I still alive."

Forcing her lips straight, she pushed away the smile that tugged at her lips. "Still, this is all about you, don't you think you should stay?"

"Yvonne, these people in here all grown—they don't need me to look after dem."

Looking around at the many people studying the displays, a sudden feeling of guilt left her feeling empty. The idea that he only wanted to leave because of her made her insides disappear, leaving only an empty shell.

"Stop worry 'bout other people." No one else would have noticed the potency in his words, the sudden change to his voice that made them sound more powerful. Yvonne noticed, like she noticed the conviction in his tone that made her guilt retreat like an ebbing tide. "What do *you* want?"

She knew what answer to give and did so without hesitation. "I want to leave."

The sternness that had made his face slightly severe instantly melted into a broad smile before he crooked his elbow. "Let's go."

After a last glance at her idol image, she took his arm and strolled with him the way they had come.

This time, when they met Jonathan, her confidence was such that she could hold his gaze during their brief conversation before Garvey confirmed that he would talk to him soon. Her initial worry about him seeing what she looked like naked was no longer a concern.

As they approached the door, Garvey released Yvonne, sliding his arm down her back to let it settle at her waist to guide her through the door that was too narrow for both of the couple at the same time.

Stepping out onto the dark side street, Yvonne turned around to find that the artist had been accosted by a fan just before he followed her through the door. She smiled as a light breeze caught her hair and laid it across her face, proud of the success he had achieved. Pushing her hair back, she caught sight of the same poster she had seen when she arrived, one advertising the exhibition with Garvey's name taking pride of place.

Seeing him beyond the glass, a sudden desire to let everyone know that she was with him widened her smile.

"It really is a fantastic exhibition, Garvey." Yvonne offered the compliment as he walked through the door, suddenly conscious of the fact that she had yet to give him her opinion. "You should be so proud of yourself."

He stopped directly in front of her, close enough for their bodies to touch but leaving a minute gap. "Thank you," he smiled, still modest. "Are you proud of me?"

"Of course," she asserted. "I love my mural, but all your other work is just so good, so inspiring."

"That's enough for me."

Casually glancing back and forth, he gave the impression that his words were throwaway, but that didn't prevent her yearning to throw her arms around him. Resisting the temptation, she settled for gazing at the look of innocence on his young face.

Returning his hand to the small of her back, Garvey directed her towards the main road. "This way, we can hail a cab."

"You don't seem very excited by it all." Looking up at him, she allowed herself to be led. "It is a great achievement."

"I know it is, and I'm proud of every single piece, but everything in there is done, it's past. When you finish a book, do you dwell on it or move on to the next story?"

Rather than wait for a response, he left her to ponder the question as he stepped off the kerb, almost walking into the path of a taxi, its orange light shining through the darkness.

The driver pulled up next to him, aligning the door with where Garvey stood, allowing him to open the door and usher her in.

Offering no objection when he gave the driver her address, she was quietly pleased that he hadn't suggested his flat. She had been there once before and found it to be an extended art studio, creating a need to step over paints, canvases and other supplies to get from one side of the room to the other.

"I get excited about the right things," he continued.

Having thought the conversation was over, she was surprised by the sudden declaration, but didn't show it, remaining silent in order to hear what else he would say.

"I get excited about the next piece I'm working on. I like to concentrate on the future."

It was such a deep statement that she expected him to qualify it, looking towards him as she waited. He said nothing, returning her soft gaze as the car pulled back into the traffic.

Sitting together as though they were in a confined space, they remained pressed against each other and left the majority of the seat free. The fact that he failed to move from the cosy position wasn't enough to leave her completely satisfied. The question on her mind made her stomach churn, unsure of whether her throat would allow her to utter the words. After a several minutes of only hearing the faint strains of the world beyond the car windows, she quietly asked, "What does your future hold?"

His slight, lopsided smile was no less powerful for it size, coming as he crossed his arm over her lap. Turning towards her, he grasped her outer thigh to pull her closer, as if their existing embrace was insufficient.

Pressing his mouth to her neck, his hot breath bathed her neck as he gradually moved upwards. "Your question should be what *your* future holds." His whispered voice heightened her curiosity, leaving her eager to hear the secretive words that would follow.

Filling her lungs, she held her breath as she waited, the seconds that passed leaving her on the verge of asking the question.

After pressing a soft kiss to the back of her ear, he continued to hover and briefly sucked her lobe before his whispered words continued, "Your future involves being undressed."

Shermaine Williams

His hand smoothly moved up her thigh, a touch that made her slowly release the breath she held. He reached beneath her coat and up to her hip, pressing firmly enough to pull her even closer to him. The pounding of her heart quickened, continuing with its rapid, deep pace even when he withdrew his hand.

Transferring his attention to her coat, he slowly loosened each button in turn. "All your clothes removed from your body, possibly nice and slow, possibly ripped off in the heat of passion."

She watched his face as he followed the deft movement of his fingers, only looking back into her eyes upon releasing her from the confines of her coat. With a single, smooth motion, he slid his hand into the loosened fold, seeming to be seeking her heartbeat as he stroked the cleft between her breasts.

"Feeling hot hands on your body, fingers creeping over your skin."

His voice remained low as if he didn't want the driver to hear his words, keeping her captivated as the rumble of his voice vibrated through to her core.

The back of his hand followed the curve of her breast with a light touch, making her jolt by passing over her erect nipple, though barely touching her.

"Exploring every part of your body."

Tilting his head as he spoke, he feigned a kiss to her mouth before leaning back to her neck, mumbling his words as her taste became his priority.

"Finding your pleasure, making you hot."

His hand continued down to her hip, pulling to twist her body towards him, certain and demanding. Leaning in to him, she raised her leg onto his lap as she desperately sought action in line with his words.

Her heart thudded in her chest and her skin tingled with anticipation, on high alert and ready for the pleasure she knew he was capable of giving. Her breathing became laboured as her heart felt like it was about to beat its way out of her chest.

Manoeuvring her body, she positioned herself where he could reach her lips, clasping his shoulder in a fierce grip as she silently indicated her desire.

Though her jagged breaths couldn't cover the sound of the passing traffic beyond the window and the intermittent beeping from where the driver sat, Yvonne felt unaware of where they were, her craving taking control and dismissing any inhibitions she would normally have experienced.

By comparison, Garvey seemed patient and calm, only too willing to tease her further by pressing his cheek to hers. "Curious fingers and eager lips exploring your body, joined by a strong tongue."

The warm caress of his breath on her ear had as much of an effect as his words, his power over her easily demonstrated by the satisfying pulsating between her thighs. Spreading her legs did nothing to alleviate the pressure that began to build, demanding his touch with an unrelenting and spreading pulse.

The desire to satisfy the insistent yearning tugging at her walls lifted her onto his lap, her skirt riding higher as she desperately sought what she needed. Sliding her hand from his shoulder to snake around his neck, she flattened her body to his in a perfect mould. With one sharp motion, her arm continued on a route to encircle his neck in a tight clinch as she straddled his lap.

Her skirt rode higher, exposing her readiness to fuck him right there, feeling the strength of his desire by the stiffness at his crotch. He finally permitted the touch of her lips, offering his in a brief hiatus from his provocation that allowed Yvonne to suck his lower fleshy fold into her mouth. Yvonne detected a faint hint of sweetness and was on the verge of recognising the flavour when it was snatched away. Permitting nothing more, Garvey continued to hold her waist when he pulled back, making it clear that he had other ideas. Driving his chin against her jaw, her skin soft compared to the rough stroke of his, he turned her head to one side to hover his lips close to her ear. "Every touch spreading fire through your body," he whispered.

"Ah." A heavy sigh rattled from her throat, releasing the pressure that built inside her from frustrated want.

Despite his arousal, his self-control held fast, letting her work herself up into a frenzy with nothing more than his words. The ensuing silence was evidence that words weren't even necessary as she continued to rock her hips, her body clenched as she drove her pelvis against his bulge. The heavy breaths that accompanied her actions seemed to make them more intense, giving her a rush of adrenaline that made her fearless and capable of more than she ever thought possible.

Clenching her vulva as if gripping his shaft, the movement couldn't stem the tide of liquid heat that threatened to flow in a deluge. Pressure to her clit intensified the sensation like a switch had been flicked, setting a fire that burned with a passion that made her body tremble.

In the heat of the taxi, Yvonne's breath caught in her throat as her heart thumped, sending blood rushing through her veins. Though she could barely think straight, only one thing on her mind, she sensed his imminent words. She had been drawn into the picture he'd verbally painted and needed to hear more.

"I wanna taste you."

The whispered sentence was unexpected, stoking the flame inside her as she was sure was his intention. Despite their embrace, he pulled her closer as his breath bathed her neck with heat.

"When you realise that, you know what my future holds." She turned to him, kissing him hard, holding his face to demand the kiss that would prevent her from exploding.

Feeling like she was giving in to an addiction she just couldn't resist, Yvonne kissed him hungrily, forcing his tongue aside with her own as if she was powerless to do anything else.

"Here we are." The driver's voice cut through her feverish mist to confirm they had reached their destination, having been there for several long moments, ending the craven kiss by her gripping his lower lip between her teeth.

Sounding like a hiss, Garvey's sharp intake of breath came as an instant result of her action, his arm tightening around her waist.

A faint feeling of disbelief made Yvonne glance through the side window, looking back through the rear when she found her view obscured by spreading condensation and the darkness of night. The familiar sight of houses and cars she saw every day made her abandon her real disbelief, reluctantly relinquishing her position as Garvey shifted to reach for his pocket, bodily lifting her in the process.

Briefly closing her eyes, sweeping back stray strands of hair tickling her forehead, she took a deep breath in an attempt to relax. However, the thump of her heart seemed to grow stronger with one glimpse at Garvey as he engaged the driver, the aroma of her own body tickling her nostrils.

With her coat splayed open, the cool edge of the vinyl seat pressed to the back of her thighs, causing a strange feeling that she hadn't previously noticed. Shuffling forwards, the seat creaking, Yvonne pulled her skirt down to its rightful place, looking beyond the glass at her side as the headlights of a passing car swept past them, momentarily highlighting the car.

Still seized by her yearning for him, Yvonne turned back to Garvey and caught the eyes of the driver in the rear view mirror in the process, noting he hurriedly averted his gaze to resume finding change. Unfazed by his interest, or the idea that he may have glanced many more times during the journey, Yvonne could only wonder whether she would have been able to cope had every person in the gallery known that she was the model for the sculpture.

Squeezing her hand as he opened the door, Garvey dragged her from her fantasy and made her follow him out of the car. Swinging her legs out of the door that Garvey stood by, Yvonne's coat billowed out behind her as she unfurled her body from the back seat, barely taking a step before she stumbled, her arms flying out as her legs suddenly became useless.

"Whoa." His exclamation was tame and calm compared to Yvonne's short shriek, accompanying his swift movement as he formed his arm into a hook and held it beneath her body.

Recovering her footing, she found his support was unnecessary as she planted her feet firmly, attempting to regain her composure by drawing her coat around her and lifting her bag back onto her shoulder from the crook of her elbow.

"You drunk?" he asked laughingly, shoving the door closed.

Smiling back, Yvonne briefly cast her eyes downwards and shook her head. A change to the atmosphere made her look up, just in time to catch him dip to lift her. Laughter followed her shocked shriek as she was thrown over his shoulder, jogged up and down as he carried her to the front door, his hand firmly gripping both her legs.

"Garvey!" she admonished, her tone more amused than hostile as she gripped his back from her upended position, balling his jacket in her fists. "Put me down."

"I will," he confirmed. "Soon."

"I have to unlock the door." Watching the crazy paving of her own path pass beyond the flash of his striding black shoes, knowing he would have to put her down.

As he came to a halt, the rumble of a car's engine made her jump, looking up to see the cab just as it drove away before she was spun in a semicircle.

"Go ahead."

Yvonne strained to raise her upper body level with the door lock. "Are you serious?" The question came as she manoeuvred to let her bag slide down her arm, knowing she wouldn't get a response. After some awkward fumbling to find her keys, she unlocked the door and pushed it open to allow Garvey to carry her inside.

After closing the door behind them, Garvey took a couple of steps into the hallway before leaning forwards to let her frame fall into his grip, his hands clasping her waist. Pressing her back to the wall, he pinned her beneath the weight of his physique, lifting her arms to rest them on his shoulders.

"Are you trying to wrap me around you?"

A seductive smile curled her lips as she linked her arms around his neck by gripping one wrist, raising her knees either side of his waist to hold him between her legs. Taking slow, deep breaths, drawing in his scent, Yvonne let her gaze drift over his face, decorated by traces of her dark red lipstick on his mouth and high on his cheek.

"I've been wrapped in you since I first met you."

Pushing her thighs inwards, she squeezed him tighter in demonstration of her pleasure at his comment.

"So, still don't want to put me down?" she smiled, trying to recall when her lips had travelled so far across his face.

He nodded, watching her from the slits left by heavy lids. "When we get to your bed."

The couple maintained a silent embrace, each reading the face of the other well enough to negate their need for words. Yvonne could hear only her own heartbeat pounding in her ears, immediately reacting when his bulge grew and pressed between her thighs. His shaft jumped, tapping her labia as if seeking entry, which made her grip him tighter, thrusting her hips forwards.

The rumbling growl from deep in the back of his throat was delectable to Yvonne, but quickly became a frustration as it proved not to be an introduction to the kiss her parted lips yearned for.

By contrast, Garvey appeared happy to simply watch her, doing nothing more than giving her the opportunity to turn herself on whilst he remained cool.

"How can you be so patient?" she demanded in a hoarse whisper, grinding against the shaft hidden beneath the fly of his slacks. "I missed you so badly."

"Because I think ahead," he admitted. "I knew I was going to see you again."

Though she knew it smacked of desperation, the need to question what part she would play in his life needled her, but she managed to resist. Instead, she willed him to say what she thought she already knew.

He flashed his easy smile. "Our futures are laid out in front of us."

Warmth spread through the pit of her stomach, floating upwards until her chest swelled. She knew a declaration of exactly what would be part of their future was too much to ask—that wasn't his style—but what he had given her was enough. "Does that mean you're going to make good on what you started in the car?"

He snorted and shook his head. "You real demanding now—I like it." With a deep kiss, he demonstrated precisely how much he liked her suggestion, humming into her mouth as her eyes fluttered closed.

Pulling his mouth away, Garvey unceremoniously ended the kiss to leave her mouth agape. "Let's go."

Turning around and lurching forwards, he maintained his hold on her body with one arm in order to walk up the stairs. Yvonne clung to him with a grip that was more than adequate to keep her pressed to his body. Laying her head on his shoulder, she marvelled at the intensity of what she felt for him, feeling so different than how she had before he walked into her life.

"Don't feel like your work is done," he declared as they reached the top of the stairs, intruding on her thoughts.

"What work?"

Shouldering the bedroom door open, he carried her inside. "As my model. Next, I'm gon' cover you in gold leaf."

"Gold leaf? You really want me for it?"

Laying her on the bed, he stood at the foot of it to look down at her. "Of course. When you find your muse, you don't let them go."

As Yvonne watched him shrug off his jacket, liquid warmth flooding her pubis, she could only smile her complete agreement.

About the Author

In her early thirties and a born and bred Londoner, Shermaine Williams has loved reading since she was a child. She began writing relatively recently after becoming bored with the career that came after finishing university.

She writes contemporary erotic romance, telling tales of characters that she hopes people can see themselves in. She gets inspiration from the most unassuming acts that people all around her don't realise they are performing. Stories with a twist always get her attention.

In addition to fiction, she also writes other pieces that are positively mundane by comparison.

Shermaine Williams loves to hear from readers.

You can find her contact information, website details and author profile page at http://www.total-e-bound.com.

Total-E-Bound Publishing

www.total-e-bound.com

Take a look at our exciting range of literagasmic™
erotic romance titles and discover pure quality
at Total-E-Bound.